SUMMER OF THE DRAGONS

Ed Clarke

PUFFIN

PUFFIN BOOKS

UK | USA | Canada | Ireland | Australia
India | New Zealand | South Africa

Puffin Books is part of the Penguin Random House group of companies
whose addresses can be found at global.penguinrandomhouse.com.

www.penguin.co.uk
www.puffin.co.uk
www.ladybird.co.uk

First published 2020
001

Text copyright © Ed Clarke, 2020
Chapter head illustrations copyright © Simone Krüger, 2020

The moral right of the author and illustrator has been asserted

Set in 13/20 pt Bembo Book MT Std
Typeset by Jouve (UK), Milton Keynes
Printed and bound in Great Britain by Clays Ltd, Elcograf S.p.A.

A CIP catalogue record for this book is available from the British Library

ISBN: 978–0–241–36048–4

All correspondence to:
Puffin Books
Penguin Random House Children's
One Embassy Gardens, New Union Square
5 Nine Elms Lane, London SW8 5DA

For Mum and Dad

Chapter 1

Wheeeeep!

Mari Jones had two fingers in her mouth and was letting out a high-pitched whistle. One solitary cow in the herd turned round, slightly befuddled.

'She's not whistling at you, Ermintrude,' said Mari's mother, Rhian, to the bewildered beast. 'Though if you would move yourself and your friends into the next field, we would be greatly obliged.'

Mari scanned her surroundings. The creature she was calling was a good deal smaller than Ermintrude.

'Where's she gone now?' she asked.

'Chasing rabbits?' said Rhian with a wry smile. 'Border collies are a lot more reliable for this kind of work, you know.'

'I know. But show me the collie that can do *that*,' said Mari, pointing up into the sky above their heads.

Out of the spring sunshine swooped a tiny, bat-sized animal. A flash of crimson glinted in the light, spiralling around the herd, before diving down to whip through the legs of the black-and-white cows. A kind of organized chaos ensued. Bellowed complaints as hooves slipped and slid in the mud, and flanks were jostled left and right. Eventually they were all lumbering in the same direction. Apart from Ermintrude, who was now looking entirely the wrong way and paying no attention whatsoever.

The tiny bat-sized thing landed squarely on Ermintrude's nose.

'Gweeb . . .' said Mari to herself nervously.

Gweeb wasn't a bat. Or a bird. Or a flying newt. Though she looked a bit like all of those things.

'Gweeb!' shouted Mari, more urgently now.

'She wouldn't, would she?' Rhian asked her.

Gweeb stretched out her neck, opened her jaws and let out a great jet of flame over Ermintrude's head, narrowly missing her ears.

Because Gweeb was a dragon. A dragon that fitted neatly into the palm of Mari's twelve-year-old hand.

'GWEEB!' yelled Mari and Rhian together.

Ermintrude began to panic, wildly shaking her head to rid herself of the flame-breathing demon on her nose.

Mari put her fingers in her mouth to let loose another almighty whistle.

Wheeeeep!

Finally Gweeb responded, lifting lazily into the air as Ermintrude staggered gratefully away in the direction of her friends. The dragon flapped casually over to Mari's outstretched hand.

'Naughty gwiber,' said Mari, calling the dragon by her full Welsh name to show her displeasure.

Gweeb just nestled herself further into Mari's palm, stretching out her tail to wind it around Mari's little finger. Rhian rolled her eyes. The dragon knew just what to do to stop Mari being angry with her.

'OK, Gweeb, but that's the last time, all right?' said Mari.

'Border collies,' said Rhian. 'Just saying.'

'Don't listen to her, Gweeb,' said Mari. 'Mum wouldn't have it any other way.'

And she knew for sure that she wouldn't. They had all been through too much together for that.

In the year since Gweeb had come to live with them at the farm, she had become more than a pet, more than a friend; she was part of the family now. And bar a few small behavioural issues, she was pretty useful around the farm too.

'Jogger,' said Rhian suddenly.

Mari spun round to look down at the path that ran along the bottom of the field. Beyond were the cliffs, and there, pounding his way wearily from a lighthouse in the distance, was a mud-splattered middle-aged man wearing a tight fluorescent top to stop his belly from bouncing.

Mari instinctively slipped Gweeb into the pocket of her hooded top. She was used to keeping the dragon away from prying eyes. Only six people in the world knew about Gweeb. Four of them were sworn to secrecy – Mari, her mum, her best friend Dylan, and Dylan's dad (Rhian's boyfriend), Gareth the vet. Nobody believed the other two – Ffion from school, because people were used to her saying ridiculous things, and Dr Griff Griffiths, the TV palaeontologist, because everyone thought he had gone mad. And he had done a very good job of proving them right.

Dr Griff couldn't stop telling anyone who would listen that he had found a colony of real, live, tiny dragons in a cave on the Heritage Coast of the Vale of Glamorgan. And that the eleven-year-old Mari Jones knew all about it too, because one of the reptiles had become her pet. When asked by the newspapers what evidence he had to back up this sensational claim, Griff had to confess that the last he had seen of the dragons, they were all flying off into the sunset together, although Mari and her family definitely knew more than they were letting on. The more the press ridiculed him, the more he insisted he would prove it, even going so far as to park his camper van in a field next to Dimland Cross Farm in the hope of catching sight of Gweeb through his long-lensed camera. In the end, the police were called, and Griff was forbidden by a court order from coming within 100 metres of the farm – or Mari. He lost his job on the TV and any semblance of respect. Finally, after a month of hanging sulkily around Llanwerydd, his girlfriend, Nita, had persuaded him to move up to the Brecon Beacons, and that was the last anyone had heard of him.

Rhian clanged the gate shut behind the newly repositioned cows. 'I reckon we've earned a spell on the beach. Whaddya say?'

A smile spread across Mari's face. That was not a question that her mum ever needed to ask.

Chapter 2

Rhian's battered Land Rover rocked and rolled its way across the uneven field. As they finally joined a track that led down to the lighthouse, Mari noticed that her mum was looking a bit green.

'You OK, Mum?'

'Just a bit queasy. Must have eaten something that didn't agree with me this morning,' replied Rhian.

They were nearly at the cliffs now, but in the final field on their right they passed an old 4x4 pickup with a rusting hulk of a caravan attached to the rear. From the top flew a white flag with a red dragon on it. It looked a bit like the Welsh flag, except the dragon had two legs rather than four. A large woman wearing camouflage shorts and pink wellies stood at the door, holding back a bulldog that was straining at its leash.

'Calm down, Gwyneth,' said the woman, hushing the dog.

It was Petra Lunk – officially the most eccentric person in Llanwerydd . . . until Griff had come along. Petra was the kind of person who believed things most people didn't. Like the 'fact' that humans had never really been into space, and that NASA had staged all the photographs of the moon landing in a Hollywood studio. She also believed that the Loch Ness monster was a family of dinosaurs that all lived secretly at the bottom of the lake, and that the royal family was descended from a race of aristocratic aliens. However, Petra didn't believe Griff's claim that there were dragons in Llanwerydd. That idea was too crazy even for her.

Petra waved. 'Hello, ladies!'

'Hello, Petra!' shouted Mari cheerily out of the window as Rhian slowed down politely.

'Not seen any little *dragons* lately, have you?' she chuckled.

'Ha! No!' replied Mari as breezily as she could, her hand instinctively reaching for the pocket Gweeb was hiding in.

'Your secret is safe with me, ladies.' Petra winked and tapped her nose. 'Really, how dare that Griffiths man accuse you of lying about something as ridiculous as that! Everyone knows that dragons died out centuries ago.'

'Ha! Yes!' Mari could feel Gweeb's snout pushing against her hand, trying to escape.

Petra looked both ways, then whispered conspiratorially, 'You can't trust anyone on the television these days. If he comes back and bothers you again, I'll set Gwyneth on him.'

Gwyneth barked in agreement. Mari felt Gweeb flinch.

'Smile and nod,' said Rhian quietly.

'Ha!' Mari nodded. 'Thank you, Petra! Must be going! See you around!'

As Rhian put her foot on the accelerator, Mari breathed a sigh of relief and lifted her hand off her pocket. Gweeb poked her nose out.

'Do you think it's a bit risky, Mum?' said Mari. 'Taking Gweeb to the beach like this?'

'You're not worried about Petra, are you? She's too busy worrying about government cover-ups to see what's right under her nose. Besides, summer's coming. In a few weeks the beach will be too busy. We need to get down while we can.'

Mari smiled at the little creature in her lap. 'Well, just try to remember you're a secret, Gweeb.' The dragon nuzzled into Mari's finger as she stroked her head.

The Land Rover finally pulled up next to the lonely café by the lighthouse. As the summer season hadn't started yet, the place was all boarded up, but it didn't matter, because Mari and Rhian hadn't come for a cup of tea. They reached behind their seats to pull out two matching canvas rucksacks. Inside were matching sets of hammers, chisels, brushes, hard hats and goggles. They were tools for fossil hunting. Mari loved hers because being a palaeontologist was all she had ever wanted. Rhian loved hers because it was now a thing that she and Mari could do together. Many years had gone by when Mari hadn't wanted to spend time with her mother – so these moments felt extra special.

They picked their way down the beach, scanning the shoreline for any early tourists or dog-walking locals.

'Coast is clear!' announced Rhian.

Mari batted her mum playfully on the back. This had become a bit of a running joke between them. Mari had a good look in both directions herself, for good measure, then reached into her pocket.

'OK, Gweeb,' she said. 'Time to stretch your wings.'

Gweeb's snout emerged once more from Mari's hoodie, took a sniff of the sea air and nosed out into the open. A second later, the little dragon had sprung forth and rocketed off into the distance. Gweeb loved the beach almost as much as Mari did. With its slatted layers of rolling, undulating rock, it provided the perfect terrain for exhilarating, low-flying aerobatics, and the dark caves cut into the cliffs provided the perfect hiding places, should anyone appear unexpectedly –

'Hey, Mari!'

It was Geraint Sharma, a friend of Mari and Dylan's at school – though 'friend' might be stretching it. Geraint's best, and perhaps only, previous friend, Angelo Thomas, had gone to a different secondary school when they all left Llanwerydd Primary, and Geraint had rather latched on to Mari at 'big school'. Mari and Dylan had become local celebrities when they survived the cliff fall trapping them in a cave (the cave where Mari had discovered the dragons): being friends with them had helped raise Geraint's social status from 'nobody anyone noticed' to 'somebody they sort of recognized'. Which was good enough for him.

'What are you doing here, Geraint?' asked Mari, her eyes instinctively darting in the direction of

Gweeb. Geraint hadn't noticed, but off in the distance the little dragon was slaloming around some gigantic boulders by the water's edge.

'I'm in training. To be a lifeguard,' he replied.

'Aren't you a bit young for that, Geraint?' asked Rhian, seeing Mari was preoccupied.

'No, Mrs Jones,' he replied. 'I'm getting my qualifications to be in Lifeguard Support. I'll be able to save anyone under five.'

'That sounds great, Geraint,' said Mari, trying to keep an eye on Gweeb over his shoulder, 'but we really have to be going.'

'But didn't you just get here?' he asked. 'Look, I brought my binoculars. And my walkie-talkies. In case anyone needs saving.'

Geraint rummaged around in his backpack to pull out the items. Only he couldn't hold all three at once, and one of the walkie-talkies fell on to the rocks, spilling batteries everywhere.

'We'll keep our eyes peeled,' said Mari. 'For toddlers in distress.'

She made a big show of shielding her eyes with one hand and gazing into the distance, as if appreciating the sunset, though of course she was really looking for Gweeb. Finally she spotted a dark cave behind Geraint suddenly light up, as if it had been illuminated by the smallest of flames. She breathed a sigh of relief. So that was where the mischievous reptile had got to.

'It's nice to see you, Mari,' said Geraint.

'Mm-hmm,' she said, not really listening. She needed to get to the cave before Gweeb drew any more attention to herself.

'And you too, Mrs Jones,' Geraint added quickly.

'Good luck with all the training, Geraint,' said Rhian. 'I'm sure you'll be great.'

Geraint beamed, and held the binoculars up to his eyes the wrong way round.

'Ha!' he laughed nervously as he turned them the right way. 'It's harder to see things when they're small, isn't it?'

Mari smiled. *And sometimes that's just as well*, she thought.

'And then he said, "It's harder to see things when they're small"!'

Mari burst into a fit of giggles. She was telling the story of what had happened on the beach to her friend Dylan, and his father, Gareth, who had come over for dinner. Dylan rolled his eyes as he helped lay the table in the kitchen.

'It's a good job his brain is smaller than Gweeb,' said Dylan.

'Now, now,' said Mari. 'Geraint's nice – and harmless.'

Gweeb was perched on her shoulder, as she usually was around the house. 'But it is lucky you haven't got any bigger, isn't it, Gweeb?'

'Can you get some candles, Mari?' asked Rhian from the stove.

'What do we want candles for? It's only Dylan and Gareth, Mum. Like any other Sunday.'

'I think it would be nice for our guests,' said Rhian.

Mari raised her eyebrows at Dylan and Gareth, as if to remind them how honoured they should feel to receive this kind of treatment. She rummaged around in the back of the cupboard in their Welsh dresser and pulled out two candles. They didn't match – one was thick and red and the other was thin and white – but they would do. She dug out a box of matches from a drawer and began trying to strike one, without success.

Seeing Mari struggling, Gweeb swooped down from her shoulder to land on the large red candle. Before Mari could protest, she breathed out a jet of flame that not only lit the candle, but melted the top half, and very nearly set fire to the tablecloth. Dylan had to duck quickly so that his mop of tight curly hair wasn't singed.

'Gweeb!' shouted Rhian. 'What have we said about fire breathing in the house?'

Dylan and Gareth struggled to stop themselves laughing.

'She's just doing what comes naturally to her, Rhian,' said Gareth. 'At least she's not doing it in the hay barn any more.'

'She's just trying to help, Mum,' said Mari. 'Aren't you, Gweebie?'

She stroked Gweeb's snout. The dragon proudly lifted her head into Mari's touch, and curled her tail around her little finger.

'All I'm saying is, it's a dangerous thing for an animal to be doing in a house with young children,' said Rhian as she put down a steaming shepherd's pie in the middle of the table.

'We're not that young,' replied Mari.

Rhian froze, as if she'd just realized she'd said

something she shouldn't have. 'No, I know. That's not what I . . .' She shot a nervous glance at Gareth.

'N-n-no, course not,' he stammered, flushing quickly.

An awkward silence descended over the table. Mari looked from Rhian to Gareth.

'What's going on?' she asked.

'Nothing,' said Rhian, but she nervously spilled a bit of the pie on the table as she served Dylan.

'There's definitely *something* going on,' he agreed.

Rhian looked at Gareth. Gareth looked back and nodded. She took a deep breath.

'Well,' she began. 'We really wanted to tell you this later, but –'

'Tell us what?' said Mari and Dylan at exactly the same time.

'Maybe we should wait till after we've eaten,' said Rhian, still holding a spoonful of pie in her hand.

'NO!' replied Mari and Dylan.

'OK, OK.' Rhian sat down and put the spoon back in the pie dish, where Gweeb eyed it hungrily. 'This isn't something that Gareth and I planned, but we're very happy about it.'

Mari and Dylan exchanged a mystified look. Rhian glanced back over to Gareth again for reassurance. 'In a few months' time, you and Dylan –' Rhian cleared her throat – 'are going to have a little baby sister.'

Mari couldn't quite take in what she was hearing. It couldn't be true, could it? Dylan seemed as shocked as she was.

Gareth filled the deafening silence. 'Like your mum says, we're both really happy this has happened. And we hope you'll be happy about it too. So, we've been talking about how we'd like things to be now, you see, and it may seem a little quick, but we've decided we want to . . . get married. At the end of the year.'

Mari whipped her head round to see whether her mum was in agreement with this rather unexpected plan.

'That's right,' said Rhian. 'And I've asked Gareth if he and Dylan want to move in before then. As soon as they're ready to, of course. So we'll all be one family, together, here at the farm.'

Rhian smiled at Gareth and Dylan. Gareth smiled back warmly and took her hand.

'But . . . but . . .' Dylan seemed to be struggling to get his head round it too. 'The baby. When's it coming?'

'*She*,' replied Gareth. 'She'll be here at the end of September.'

'And what'll that make Mari and me?' Dylan asked. 'When you two are . . . ?'

'Well,' said Gareth, 'technically you'll be brother and sister, but –'

'Brother and sister!' exclaimed Dylan.

He and Mari sat back in their chairs, slightly shell-shocked.

'Shall we eat now?' offered Rhian, picking up the serving spoon again. 'It's going to get cold.'

Gweeb licked her lips, but food was not the uppermost thing in Mari's mind. Her brain was still whirring.

'But where is a baby going to go?' she said. 'There's no room for everyone.'

Rhian spooned a portion of the shepherd's pie on to Mari's plate. 'Well, there'll be a bit of reorganization to do, but once we clear all the boxes out of the back bedrooms you can have one of those each. Will you have some peas?'

'What?' Mari protested. 'Are you saying I can't stay in my room?'

'To begin with, yes, love, of course,' said Rhian. 'The baby will be in with us. But in six months or so she'll need a room of her own. And yours is the smallest, and the closest to my –' she glanced over at Gareth before correcting herself – '*our* bedroom. I'm sorry to move you, but it makes sense. And, you know, you're older now, Mari. You need a bigger room anyway.'

'But I *like* having a small room, Mum. And the back bedrooms are so chilly. The wind whistles right round them. And there's mould growing by the ceiling.'

'That's only because we've turned the radiators off to save money, Mari. With Gareth bringing in a salary as well as what we earn from the farm, we'll have enough to redecorate. We'll make them so cosy, I promise you. You can choose new curtains, a new carpet –'

'I don't want new curtains! And I like my carpet how it is.'

Then, to everyone's surprise, Dylan suddenly pushed back his chair with a screech and bolted out of the door.

Gareth called after him, 'Dylan, your dinner!'

Gweeb took her chance, unfurled her tongue, and snatched a pea from Mari's plate.

Mari let her knife and fork clatter to the table and ran after Dylan.

She found him sitting on a crumbling wall in the farmyard. He was picking at the loose stones and chucking them on the ground. Mari could see a tear making slow progress down his cheek. He wiped it away with the back of his hand, but it was soon replaced by a new one. Mari wandered over to slump down next to him. They sat together for a while in silence before, finally, Mari found something to say.

'Guess we should be happier than this, right?'

Dylan nodded.

'So why aren't we?'

He shrugged. They both picked up a stone and threw them at the same time.

'One minute you're having your dinner, and the next you're sitting on a wall with your new brother.'

'Yep,' agreed Dylan.

'Things were just fine how they were,' said Mari. 'Mum and I were finally getting on OK. Now it's like starting all over again.'

Dylan turned to her. 'Is that what's bothering you about all this?'

'Well, yes. Isn't it kind of the same for you?' Mari looked at him expectantly, but Dylan just stared at his feet.

Then Gweeb squeezed out of the farmhouse kitchen window and flew over to Mari's shoulder. 'Mum kick you out for eating my dinner again?'

Gweeb ambled across on to Dylan's shoulder before nestling into his neck. But just as he was reaching up to stroke her, she sprang into the air and soared high up above the house. She circled the roof a couple of times, then darted off towards a nearby overhead cable where a little bird was perched.

'She's not hungry enough to eat that bird, is she?' pondered Dylan.

Mari squinted up at the cable and her heart jumped in her chest. 'That's not a bird,' she said disbelievingly. 'That's another dragon . . .'

Chapter 4

In an instant, all thought of these changes in their own lives were forgotten – because here, right before their eyes, were *two* dragons, sitting on a wire over the farmyard like it was the most normal thing in the world.

Rhian and Gareth appeared at the kitchen door to see what they were staring at.

'Is that what I think it is?' asked Rhian.

'Mm-hmm.' Mari put her fingers to her lips, and blew a calling whistle to Gweeb. It took a moment,

25

but almost reluctantly Gweeb swooped down to her hand. They all waited with bated breath to see if the other dragon would follow, but it seemed wary. 'Grab me a worm please, Dylan,' said Mari.

He quickly turned over a stone and passed one to her. She held out her other hand, positioning the wriggling invertebrate between her thumb and forefinger. Finally the other dragon lifted off and arrowed down towards Mari's outstretched hand. Mari couldn't help a broad grin breaking out across her face. The dragon could have been Gweeb's exact double, apart from one thing – a distinctive yellow stripe above its left eye.

'It's the same dragon, Dylan,' she said. He raised a puzzled eyebrow. 'Don't you remember? The one from the cave last year. When we let them all out of the backpack, this was the first one. It curled its tail around Gweeb's and they took off together.'

Dylan smiled in recognition. So much had happened that day – the rockfall, getting trapped in the cave with Griff, being rescued by their parents – but the most joyous part of all had been seeing all those tiny dragons they'd found in the cave flying free.

'So they know each other already?' asked Rhian.

Mari and Dylan both nodded.

'But what we don't know is why you've come back, Mr Stripe,' said Mari. 'And what happened to the rest of your family?'

'You sure it's a boy this time?' said Dylan with a wink. It was an in-joke between him and Mari, as they had both thought Gweeb was a boy dragon at first.

The striped dragon had now curled its tail around Gweeb's and the pair were snuggled up contentedly on Mari's right hand.

'I have a hunch.' She grinned. 'Let's assume he is until we know different. Is that OK with you, Mr Stripe?'

'We can't call him Mr Stripe,' Dylan protested. 'It sounds like a clown who does kids' birthday parties.'

'OK, well, maybe just Stripe then.'

'More importantly,' said Rhian, 'how are we going to keep *two* dragons secret?'

27

The dragons sprang off Mari's hand and darted into the air, chasing each other across the roof like swallows. It was a sight to marvel at, but Mari couldn't help feeling a little bewildered at the same time. There was so much happening at once.

'Maybe we could train him, like we did with Gweeb,' Dylan suggested. But even as he spoke, Stripe suddenly seemed to catch a scent of something, and shot off in a new direction, with Gweeb in hot pursuit.

Mari realized instantly where he was heading. 'The cows!'

When Gweeb had first arrived at the farm, it became very clear, very quickly, that she really, really loved milk. Being the son of a vet, Dylan had known that it wasn't a good idea for reptiles to drink milk, which was really food for mammals. But Gweeb didn't seem to care about that, and whenever she drank it, she tended to go slightly manic – like a toddler who's eaten too many sweets. Mari had managed to train her not to chase the cows, after she once bit one on the udder while trying to drink its milk, but Stripe didn't have that training . . .

Mari raced towards the herd and swung herself over the gate in one vaulting move. She squelched through the mud, her trainers getting caked, fearing the worst. But her worries were entirely misplaced. Stripe wasn't hassling the cows at all, but racing Gweeb through the legs of the cattle, as playful as a butterfly. Whenever he looked like he was being tempted by a dangling udder, Gweeb would swoop down in front of him and make him chase her again.

Dylan soon arrived on the scene, followed not long after by an out-of-breath Rhian and Gareth.

'What happened?' asked Dylan.

'Gweeb's guarding the herd,' said Mari with a proud smile. 'We'll make a farmer of her yet.'

She felt her mum's arm round her shoulders as Gareth put his arm round Dylan's. The four of them stood and watched the tiny red dragons play as if they didn't have a care in the world. And, for that fleeting moment, neither did they.

Chapter 5

'Has anyone seen Gweeb and Stripe?' asked Mari as she wrestled a cardboard box up the stairs.

'No,' came a disjointed chorus of replies. Rhian and Gareth were manoeuvring a bed out of the back of a small rented van, and Dylan was coming downstairs to grab another load. Barely two months had passed since the news about the baby, and already Dylan and Gareth were moving into the farmhouse.

'Do you need some help with that?' asked Dylan.

'I . . . can . . . manage,' said Mari, dropping the heavy box on the landing. 'Is that your rock collection in there?'

'Not everyone has a rock collection, Mari,' replied Dylan. 'That's my books and stuff.'

He lifted out an old photo of a beautiful black woman with clever, laughing eyes. Mari recognized her immediately. It was Dylan's mum, who had died when he was little.

'Though some stuff means more than the rest,' he continued quietly, replacing the photo.

They took hold of either end of the box and hoisted it up. They wobbled along the landing to a freshly painted room at the end. Dumping the box on the newly carpeted floor, they collapsed in a heap with their backs against a radiator.

'Gweeb doesn't normally go off by herself, does she?' asked Dylan.

'No,' said Mari. 'But since Stripe got here, I can never seem to find them.'

'And that doesn't worry you?'

'I trust Gweeb,' replied Mari. 'She knows to stay away from strangers. She's already stopped Stripe buzzing the postman about three times. They're usually just off playing in a tree somewhere. I guess she's just making the most of having a new friend.'

'Are you sure you're OK with that, Rhian?'

It was Gareth, backing into the room with one end of Dylan's bed.

'I'm pregnant, not feeble,' she said, appearing round the door with the other end. 'And *you've* still got homework to do before school tomorrow,' she added, looking pointedly at Mari and Dylan.

They both sighed at the same time. 'Really, Mum? We're *so* tired from all this carrying and stuff,' Mari protested.

'Work doesn't stop on a farm just because you're tired, kids,' said Rhian with a smile, plonking the bed down.

Dylan didn't seem amused. 'Well, maybe this farm will be different, Mrs Jones,' he said sulkily, remaining resolutely glued to the floor.

'You don't have to call me Mrs Jones any more, Dylan. You can call me Rhian if you like.'

He raised his head briefly, but he didn't respond.

'Dylan,' said Gareth, putting an arm round Rhian, 'I think you should go do your homework now.'

'Come on, Dylan,' Mari said, 'before she tells the story about how she was stacking hay bales the night before she gave birth to me.'

'I think *my* mum was probably stacking shelves, but sure,' muttered Dylan as he reluctantly pulled himself to his feet. 'But I'm getting my terrarium first.'

'Fine,' said Gareth. 'But then homework, OK?'

'Fine,' echoed Dylan.

Mari followed him down the stairs. 'Everything all right?'

'Why wouldn't it be?' he shot back.

If it wasn't all right, Dylan wasn't saying why. As they emerged into the farmyard, Gweeb landed on Mari's shoulder, while Stripe landed on Dylan's. Stripe gently butted his head into Dylan's neck. Dylan raised his hand to stroke the little dragon.

'Aha!' said Mari to Gweeb. 'So, you've finally come to help then?'

'Yep, you can help us carry this,' said Dylan, leaning into the back of the van and whipping a blanket off a big glass tank.

Both the dragons instantly flew back up into the air to perch on a gutter.

'Don't think Gweeb fancies getting stuck in there again,' said Dylan, remembering how they had used a terrarium to hide her not long after Mari first found her.

'Well, they'd better stop flying off quite so much, or otherwise –' she lifted the lid – 'it's dragon jail for the both of you!'

The dragons took off in a fright.

'I was only joking!' she called after them.

'So, you two are, like, living in the same house now?'

It was Geraint Sharma again. Monday afternoon at Llanwerydd Secondary School, and they were all sitting at the back of the class in Madame Thierry's French lesson. As in most of the other lessons they shared, Geraint had elbowed his way into sitting as close to Mari as possible.

'*As-tu des frères ou des sœurs?*' called out Madame Thierry.

No one in the class was paying attention, of course.

'Yes,' whispered Mari back to Geraint.

'Ffion Jenkins, *as-tu des frères ou des sœurs?*'

In the corner a girl with dyed red hair stiffened to attention. It was Ffion Jenkins, Mari's former nemesis. Last year Ffion had been the class queen bee, making Mari's daily life a misery. Ffion had dragon-napped Gweeb and taken her into school, where Gweeb accidentally burned down the sports hall. But having her hair singed by a tiny dragon, and then being ridiculed for claiming dragons might exist, had stopped Ffion in her bossy tracks. Unlike Dr Griff, she had learned quickly to keep quiet about it all. These days she was a shadow of her former annoying self, and the only thing anyone noticed about her was her constantly changing hair colour.

'What? *Non*,' said Ffion.

'In the same bedroom?' asked Geraint.

'No!' Mari and Dylan replied at the same time, rather too loudly.

'Mari Jones!' Madame Thierry shouted. *'As-tu des frères ou des sœurs?'*

Mari froze.

'She's asking if you have any brothers or sisters,' hissed Geraint.

'I know what she's asking,' she hissed back.

But she couldn't bring herself to say it out loud. It was still too soon, too strange. Dylan glanced at her sharply, like he was wondering how she was going to reply. Some of the other kids in the class began to turn their heads too. Mari felt their laser-guided stares burn into her.

'Pour la dernière fois, alors,' said Madame Thierry, somewhat exasperated. *'As-tu, Mari, des frères ou des sœurs?'*

'Elle a un frère, Madame,' said Geraint quickly. *'Il s'appelle Dylan.'*

Geraint had clearly thought he was doing the right thing in helping Mari out. But the effect was not what he had expected. A murmur ran around the class. Then someone at the back muttered under their breath, 'Yeah, right. They could be twins!'

The whole class collapsed into fits of laughter, and both Mari and Dylan went bright red. Geraint seemed to have no idea what was happening, but the fact that he'd caused whatever it was made him go bright red too. The only person not laughing was Ffion. She just stared at the ceiling.

Before Madame Thierry could ask what was going on, the last bell rang and the class poured out of school.

The bus ride back from school was awkward. It was the first time Mari and Dylan had taken the same bus home, and a few of their classmates were sitting at the back sniggering again. Mari got on first and sat down. As Dylan followed, she opened her mouth to call him over, but he turned aside and sat across the aisle from her, three rows forward, which only made their classmates cackle more loudly. All the way home

Mari wished the scratchy blue upholstery would swallow her up.

Finally Dylan dinged the bell for their stop, and got up to wait by the door as the bus slowed down.

'Bye, Dylan!' came the shout from the back of the bus.

Mari closed her eyes and waited until the last possible moment to get up and make a dash for the door.

'BYE, MARI!'

Mari didn't turn round. She looked straight down at the floor, hustled along the aisle and leaped out of the open door.

She caught Dylan up as they walked along the lane to the farmhouse. 'Are you OK?' she asked, reaching out to touch his arm.

'Why wouldn't I be?' he replied, shrugging her off.

They walked together in silence, Mari not knowing what more to say.

As soon as they turned the last corner in the lane, she realized that something wasn't right. Rhian was waiting for them in the farmyard.

'It's Gweeb and Stripe,' she said urgently. 'They've been gone for hours.'

Mari's heart pounded. 'When was the last time you saw them?' she asked quickly.

'They flew off into the garden after lunch,' said Rhian. 'Then I started doing something else and –'

'They've always come back before though, right?' said Dylan, cutting in.

'Yes, but after, like, half an hour,' said Mari. 'And they're usually just up in the trees at the end of the garden.'

'I checked there already,' said Rhian. 'And I've been out to the field with the herd.'

Mari frowned. That left one obvious place.

'We need to get down to the beach,' she announced. 'Right now.'

Rhian's battered Land Rover slunk slowly past the caravan site by the lighthouse. They were trying to draw as little attention to themselves as possible in the hope that Petra Lunk wouldn't spot them and come out for another chat. They parked behind the little café and quietly opened and shut the car doors.

They slipped down the grassy slope to the beach and scanned the horizon for tiny flying creatures, but there were none to be seen. Just a couple of wheeling gulls – two bright white commas on the sky's darkening page. The whole beach was empty.

'We need to check the caves,' announced Mari.

Rhian shook her head. 'I don't think that's a good idea.'

After what happened last year, the caves along their stretch of coast were out of bounds for Mari and Dylan. Just a little further down the beach in the direction of Llanwerydd lay the cave where they and Griff had been trapped before a second rockfall threw them into the sea. If Rhian and Gareth hadn't arrived in the nick of time to rescue them from the waves . . . well, it didn't bear thinking about.

But it was also the cave where they had found the clutch of dragon eggs that Stripe had hatched out of. Had he and Gweeb gone back there, perhaps?

'Mum, I know what you're thinking, but this is an emergency.'

'They could be anywhere, Mari,' replied Rhian. 'There's no sense in putting yourselves at risk.'

'*Please*, Mum.'

Mari could feel the anxiety building inside her. She hadn't been apart from Gweeb this long since the time Ffion had stolen her. And that had nearly ended in the school burning down. It had started to rain now, plastering her hair to the side of her face. Mari knew she must have looked pathetic, but it did the trick.

'Stay here,' said Rhian finally. '*I'll* check the caves.'

'But you don't know them like we do, Mrs Jones,' protested Dylan.

'Dylan. First of all, you can call me Rhian, and second, you are *not* going into those caves,' she said firmly. 'I mean it. Mari, make sure he doesn't follow me.'

Dylan folded his arms and plonked himself down on a rock. 'Whatever,' he said.

Rhian looked like she was about to say something else, but then just turned and set off towards the nearest cave. Mari watched her disappear into the dark mouth cut out of the rock, the beam of her phone torch waving in front of her. Now she was worried about the dragons *and* her mum.

Then, all of a sudden, a loud bark echoed from the cave. A few seconds later, Rhian backed out of the darkness looking shaken. A bulldog came bounding after her, jumping up in a way that seemed quite threatening.

'Gwyneth!' called a voice from within the cave. As the voice's owner emerged from the gloom, pink wellies gleaming, Mari's stomach lurched. It was Petra Lunk. Rhian was trying not to look fazed by the hulking dog.

'She's just playing,' said Petra as Gwyneth circled Rhian's legs menacingly.

'What are you doing in the caves, Petra?' asked Mari. 'You know they aren't stable.'

'Mari, I appreciate your concern, but any rocks falling on my head will come off worse.' She knocked on her head with her fist. 'One hundred per cent Welsh steel plate. Doctors put it in after I had an argument with a telegraph pole. I'm more at risk from the rain than the rocks. I don't want to rust.'

'So, I think we need to go now, kids,' said Rhian, trying to hustle them back up the beach.

'But, Mum,' protested Mari, 'we haven't done . . . what we came to do.'

'What *did* you come to do on the beach in the rain?' asked Petra, her eyes narrowing.

Mari looked at her mum and Dylan, hoping they would come up with a good explanation.

'We've lost an animal,' said Dylan.

'An animal?' asked Petra, slightly suspiciously.

'Yes, a cow,' replied Rhian quickly.

'From the farm,' said Mari.

Petra cocked her head to one side. 'Do they often escape to the beach? Cows?'

'Only when they fancy a holiday,' said Rhian.

'I didn't know that about cows. Something else *they* keep quiet.'

'*They?*' asked Mari.

'The *government*,' whispered Petra, as if that explained everything.

'I really think we have to go now, kids,' said Rhian. 'Maybe that . . . cow has already gone back to the farm.'

Mari kicked a rock in frustration. But she knew that with Petra on the beach there was no way they could risk luring the dragons out into the open, even if they could find them.

The rain was coming down stronger by the time they made it back to the Land Rover, and they jumped in without a second thought. They could hear the drops hammering on the roof so hard it felt like they were trying to break in.

'There was nothing else we could do,' said Rhian. 'We don't know they were in the caves anyway. I'm sure they'll be back at the farm by now.'

Mari wasn't so certain about that, but she knew there was no point in hanging around. Rhian put the key in the ignition, turned over the engine and set the windscreen wipers going. She let off the handbrake, turned to look over her shoulder to reverse and –

'Gweeb!'

It was Mari, pointing at the windscreen wipers with glee. There, riding the blades as if they were some kind of fairground attraction, were Gweeb and Stripe. Back and forth, up and down they slid across the window, having the time of their lives.

'You two,' said Mari, with a relieved smile, 'are *double* trouble.'

'Quick,' said Rhian suddenly. 'Petra's coming.'

Mari dashed out into the rain and scooped up the little dragons before diving back into the car.

'Did she see anything?' asked Rhian, the car wheels spinning as they made their getaway.

'I don't think so, no.'

Mari turned to look out through the back window and saw the pink-wellied figure receding into the distance. Petra Lunk was standing stock still, hands on hips, staring after them.

Mari gnawed her lip anxiously. It was dark and wet, and she had got the dragons into the car in a matter of seconds. Petra couldn't have seen anything.

Could she?

Chapter 7

Bang! Bang! Bang!

Rhian hammered the final nails into a large wire-mesh-covered structure in the old farmhouse kitchen garden. It looked like the big bird cages you see at the zoo.

'There,' she said. 'I think that should do it.'

Mari wasn't happy about this, but she knew they couldn't have Gweeb and Stripe flying off to the beach by themselves any more. With the summer tourists about to arrive and Petra Lunk already suspicious, it was too risky. She ducked her head, walked through the door of the aviary, opened her hands and let the two little dragons out.

'Welcome to your new home, guys,' she said, trying to put a brave face on things. Gweeb and Stripe looked back at her, their big green eyes seeming to plead with her not to do this. The looks wrenched at her heart. It really did feel like putting them in dragon jail.

Dylan was standing outside, his fingers curled round the wire. 'It's not right,' he said, echoing her thoughts. 'They're wild creatures.'

'I know, Dylan,' said Rhian gently. 'But it's for their own good.'

His fingers gripped the mesh tighter. 'Who are you to say what's good for them, Mrs Jones?' he snapped. 'What do you know?'

'Dylan!' said Mari in surprise. 'Mum's only trying to help. And you know you don't have to keep calling her Mrs Jones.'

Dylan kicked the bottom of the aviary in frustration and stomped back into the house.

'He's in a funny mood,' said Mari. 'I'm sorry, Mum.'

'You don't have to apologize for him, Mari. There's a lot going on for Dylan, what with the move and everything. Let's go back inside.'

'I'm just going to stay here for a bit longer,' said Mari. 'To keep them company.'

Rhian smiled. 'Of course, love. Red pasta in half an hour though, OK?'

Mari nodded and stepped back out of the aviary, closing the door firmly behind her. She put her finger through one of the little wire hexagons, and waited for Gweeb to fly over to the other side, her talons grasping the metal. Her tail curled plaintively around Mari's protruding index finger. Mari sighed. But this was the way it had to be.

'Have a great summer, Mari!'

School was finished finally, and Geraint Sharma was following Mari and Dylan towards the bus stop as hordes of excited kids swarmed around them. 'Will you be down the beach?'

'I guess I'll be there at some point.'

'Would be great to, you know, get an ice cream together?' said Geraint.

'Thanks, but I'm trying not to eat too much sugar,' replied Dylan.

'I didn't mean . . .'

'Come on, Mari,' said Dylan, hustling her away.

'I don't need a bodyguard, Dylan,' she said when they were out of Geraint's earshot.

'But he wants to hang out with you *all the time*,' he said as they stepped up on to their bus. 'Isn't that a bit weird?'

'He's just lonely since Angelo went back to Cardiff.'

They sat down next to each other. The other kids on the bus didn't bother teasing them any more. It had only taken a month for them to get bored of it. Mari and Dylan living together was just how things were now.

For Mari and Dylan, it wasn't quite normal yet though. Years of living with just her mum had got Mari used to her own space, her own way of doing things. And though they might have had an extra bedroom, they certainly didn't have an extra bathroom. So coming out of the one they did have, first thing in the morning, to find a bleary-eyed Dylan waiting on the landing in his faded Cardiff City boxer shorts was something she still found quite strange.

Dylan also had some unexpected habits that took a bit of getting used to. Like using a butter knife to scrape the mud off his football boots, or absent-mindedly letting his finger wander up his nose in front of the TV in the evening. And then there was his dad's tendency to sing opera in the bath, and keep his fishing-bait maggots in a Tupperware box in the fridge. The farmhouse was certainly not what it used to be.

When they got back to the house, Mari and Dylan did what they always did, and went to check on Gweeb and Stripe. And, as the dragons always did, they both flung themselves against the mesh, with Stripe playfully banging his head against the wire across the door.

'All right, all right,' said Mari, opening it. 'Is that a thing all male creatures do, do you think? Butting their head against things?'

'*I* don't, if that's what you're asking.'

Mari shrugged. 'If you say so.'

'It's worm o'clock!' said Dylan, ignoring her.

The dragons feasted on the wriggly treats that Mari had brought in a butter tub.

'Right, time for some exercise,' she announced, holding out her hand for Gweeb to jump on to. Stripe flew straight to Dylan's shoulder. They all knew the drill.

Though Gweeb had successfully trained Stripe not to bother the cows, he still wasn't good at returning to a whistle. Or doing *anything* he was asked to, in fact. They had been trying to train him for weeks now, but he just couldn't seem to stop himself getting distracted by something or other. Sometimes it was Gweeb, sometimes a squirrel, sometimes a particularly colourful flower. Mari the scientist wondered whether this was because it was harder to train an animal the older they got. Dylan, the son of a vet, thought that animals had different characters, just like people had.

The friends stood at opposite ends of the farmyard in the warm afternoon sun, Dylan holding Gweeb, Mari holding Stripe. Mari whistled, and immediately Gweeb sprang out of Dylan's grip and swooped over to Mari's hand, where she was rewarded with a worm and a stroke on the snout. Next, Dylan gave a shrill whistle, and Mari held out her hand to encourage Stripe to go to him. Stripe just looked up at her as if to ask what on earth that terrible noise was for. Dylan tried again. This time Gweeb flew to his hand instead.

'Thank you, Gweeb,' he said. 'At least *someone* is listening to me.'

'Let's try again!' Mari shouted to him.

Again, Dylan put two fingers to his lips and blew out a high-pitched whistle. Mari pretty much threw Stripe into the air, where he seemed to hover, bemused, for a while before flitting up to a phone wire to chat to a resting blackbird. The bird flew away in shock as the bright red reptile landed next to it, and Gweeb went up to join her friend. They wrapped their tails around one another as they rocked back and forth.

Mari sighed. 'At least they're happy, I suppose,' she said, looking up at the two little dragons.

'Well, they're happy when they're out of dragon jail,' said Dylan, joining her.

She nodded sadly. 'And here comes the other contented couple.'

Gareth's bright yellow car crunched up the lane to come to a halt next to them in a swirl of dust.

'Sorry we're late on your last day!' said Rhian, climbing gingerly out of the passenger seat. Her baby bump was so big now that she had to manoeuvre herself very carefully in tight spaces. 'We got stuck in traffic at Culverhouse Cross. Can you give us a hand?'

Gareth had already opened up the back of the car and was sliding out a large flat box.

'Will you help us put it together, kids?' he asked. Rhian smiled her encouragement.

Mari looked at the picture on the box. It was a cot. 'We're just, you know, in the middle of something right now,' she said. 'With Gweeb and Stripe.'

'Many hands make light work?' Rhian tried again.

'Too many cooks spoil the . . . cot?'

Rhian's face fell a little and Mari felt bad. She knew her mum and Gareth were trying to get her and Dylan involved in the preparations for the baby, but it all still felt weird somehow. A dragon she could deal with. But a baby? She still hadn't really got her head around two boys sharing the house with them. How was she supposed to deal with a baby? A cute and shiny new girl forcing her out of her bedroom . . .

Mari glanced over at Dylan. He was purposefully ignoring the conversation, focused on scrabbling in the dirt to find a worm treat for his dragon.

On cue, Gweeb flew to Mari's shoulder. Somehow she always seemed to know when Mari wasn't feeling quite right.

'OK, I can see you're busy right now,' said Rhian. 'But don't be too long – we're going to The Lighthouse for dinner to celebrate the first day of the holidays!'

'Last day of free childcare, more like!' snorted Gareth.

Rhian clipped him round the back of the head. 'So be ready to head out at six thirty.'

At 6:15 Mari and Dylan finally shut the door of the aviary, leaving Gweeb and Stripe inside. The dragons weren't happy. At this point they would normally come into the house and spend the evening with them.

'It's just for a couple of hours,' said Mari. 'We'll be back to let you out soon enough.'

As she went up to her room to change, she caught a glimpse of something bright and white standing in Rhian and Gareth's bedroom. The newly assembled cot. Rhian came round the door and caught her staring.

'Come and have a look?' she asked.

Mari shook her head and hurried into her room.

Rhian followed her. 'Is everything OK, Mari?'

Mari didn't look round. She just nodded and busied herself with digging out fresh clothes. 'I don't have to wear anything posh, do I?'

Rhian smiled. 'It's only The Lighthouse, love.'

'I'll be down in a minute then.'

'There's no rush, Mari. Like I say, it's only The Lighthouse.'

'It feels like there's a rush, Mum. It feels like everything's happening really quickly.'

Rhian came into the room and gave her a hug. 'Sometimes we can't choose the way things happen, love. We just have to let those things carry us along.'

'I'm OK, Mum, really. You don't have to fuss.'

Rhian nodded, and was about to leave when she seemed to have second thoughts and turned back. 'It'll be good to have another girl around the house, won't it?' she said hopefully.

Mari suddenly imagined that white cot standing where her bed was now. Saw her fossils all replaced by fluffy toys.

She put on her bravest smile. 'Yes, Mum.'

Rhian left the room. A moment later, Dylan swung his head round the door. 'Ready?'

'Not really,' she replied. 'You?'

He shrugged. 'Same. Let's play happy families, shall we?'

Mari smiled at him. Whatever she was feeling, he was feeling something too. Even if she wasn't entirely sure it was the same thing.

Chapter 8

'*All'alba vincerò!*'

Gareth was singing opera, in Italian, very loudly, as they made their way back from their evening at the pub.

'*Vincerò!*'

He was getting even louder. Rhian winced as she looked over from the driver's seat.

'*VIN-CER-Ò!*'

The kids put their fingers in their ears at the same time.

'*Dah duh der duh der dah der doh . . .*'

Gareth was conducting an imaginary orchestra now. Mari and Dylan looked at each other and burst out laughing.

'There is nothing funny about Luciano Pavarotti, kids,' said Gareth. 'He was one of the greatest singers who ever lived.'

'We weren't laughing at him, Dad,' said Dylan. 'We were laughing at the person trying to sing like him.'

'So very harsh my boy is with me, Rhian,' said Gareth with a wink, looking to her for support. '*You* appreciate my talent, now, don't you?'

Rhian put on the handbrake as they pulled up at the farm. Before Gareth could start singing again, Mari and Dylan threw open the doors and rushed over to the aviary to bring Gweeb and Stripe into the house for the night.

'I'm more of a Tom Jones kind of girl, to be fair,' Mari could hear her mum saying.

'Can you see them?' asked Dylan. They were inside the aviary now. 'Use the light on your phone.'

'Oh,' said Mari suddenly. 'That isn't good.'

She was pointing down into the bottom right corner – where the light from her phone torch illuminated a hole with blackened scorch marks around it.

It wasn't a big hole, but it was big enough for two dragons to get through.

And the aviary was empty.

Twenty minutes later, Gareth's car pulled up by the café next to the beach. They had all donned wellies and warm coats, picked up a torch each, and gone straight back out. Fortunately it was late enough, and dark enough, to make it unlikely that Petra Lunk was out and about. They all slipped down the grassy slope to the shore quickly and quietly. Their torch beams criss-crossed in search of something tiny and red, but the only things they caught in the light were a couple of frightened bats.

'I think we should head towards Llanwerydd,' said Mari.

'I'm not sure that's a good idea,' said her mum, eyeing the approaching waves. The coves further along the shore were probably only twenty minutes away from being cut off by the tide.

'We'll be quick,' said Mari. 'Follow me.'

She marched off purposefully, leaving the others trailing in her wake. With only a torch and the moonlight to see by, Mari had to switch between pointing the torch at the rocks she was clambering over so she didn't fall, and the cliffs above her where she thought Gweeb and Stripe might be hiding. It was an awkward, inefficient process. After a while she stopped and tried a different tactic. She put two fingers to her mouth and blew out her calling whistle. Soon Dylan was next to her doing the same thing.

'Gweeb! Stripe!' they shouted together.

Still nothing.

Mari swung her torch like a searchlight across the face of the cliffs, but all she could see was an enormous mound of rocks spilling out of a deep black cave. She gave a little shudder. She knew that cave very well. It was the very one she and Dylan had been trapped in last year.

Neither of them had been back inside since that day. It would have meant ignoring the very large police DANGER signs warning that what was left of the cave might collapse at any minute; then clambering high over those loose rocks; peeling back the chicken wire that had been put there to stop anyone foolish enough to ignore the signs; and squeezing in through the narrow gap left at the top.

Mari tried her whistle again, and shone her torch up at the dark hole.

And suddenly a glimpse of red reflected back at her.

'Did you see that?' she asked Dylan.

'See what?'

And then there was a flash of light from *inside* the cave, only for a second.

'That!'

Mari didn't wait. She was already halfway up the scree, little bits of rock slipping away beneath her scrambling feet.

'Mari! Stop!' called Rhian.

'They're in there, Mum,' she yelled back.

Dylan followed Mari up the rocks, and Rhian and Gareth gave chase.

'Then we should wait for them to come out by themselves!' shouted Rhian. 'It's too dangerous!'

'There's something going on in there,' said Mari. 'I'm going to find out what it is!'

Behind them the water was beginning to lap at the base of the rockfall. Rhian lost her footing briefly and slipped down the slope a little. Gareth helped her back up. Before long, Mari had reached the chicken wire. The holes in the mesh were bigger than the ones in the aviary. The dragons could easily slip through, but she would have to roll it back to get inside herself. She was careful not to catch her fingers on the sharp wiry edges. Dylan arrived to help her, and then they were inside. They pointed their torch beams into the dark recess of the cave.

'Gweeb!' Mari cried. 'Where are you?'

A flash of red. Mari whipped her torch round to follow it. Then another flash, and another. Dylan tried to follow it too. Their torch beams danced around the space, trying to catch sight of whatever it was. Or whatever *they were*, because all of a sudden there was a flapping mass of red in front of their eyes, like a host of butterflies that had all taken off at the same time.

The cave was *full* of dragons.

'Oh. My. God.' Mari and Dylan said it at almost exactly the same time. They slowly swept their torches across the cave to take in the full majesty of what they were witnessing. Half the flock were in flight, the other half dotted around various perches. They could only be the dragon hatchlings they'd released last year from the very same cave. And right there, at the very front, was –

'Gweeb!'

If they hadn't been careful, they might have trodden on her.

'Stripe!' said Dylan as the little boy dragon landed on his shoulder.

Mari bent down to pick up Gweeb, but she seemed reluctant to climb on to her hand.

'Come on, Gweeb,' urged Mari. 'We don't have much time.'

She reached out for the dragon instead, gently pinning her wings to her body in order to lift her up, but Gweeb shrank away from her touch, tugging in the opposite direction.

'What's the matter with you, little Gweeb?'

'Mari!'

It was her mum calling to her, and she and Gareth were squeezing through the chicken wire.

Mari knew they had to get a move on. 'Sorry about this, but we have to go,' she said, grabbing the dragon more firmly this time. She could feel her squirming and wriggling, trying desperately to escape. And then, when Mari lifted Gweeb up, she realized why the dragon had been resisting so strongly.

'It can't be . . .' she gasped.

'What is it?' said Dylan.

There, beneath Gweeb, lay a perfectly formed, tiny, reddish-brown egg.

Chapter 9

'Gweeb laid an egg?'

Dylan was incredulous.

'Gweeb did what?' asked Rhian as she lumbered down into the cave, closely followed by Gareth. 'Hang on, what on earth is all this?'

She had finally seen the flock of dragons flapping about her like seagulls around a tractor.

Finally Mari realized what was really going on in the cave, and why half the dragons were rooted to their perches, and the other half were flying around, trying to distract the intruders.

'The dragons have come back to nest. The females are all incubating eggs,' she said. 'And the males are trying to protect them.'

'By God, you're right,' said Gareth, bending down to examine a nearby dragon. 'How marvellous.'

'It is, but we have to go now,' said Rhian. 'The tide's almost at the mouth of the cave. We'll be cut off in minutes.'

'OK, let's go, Gweeb,' said Mari, reaching down to pluck Gweeb's egg off the rock beneath her.

'Don't touch it!' said Gareth quickly.

'What do you mean?' she said.

'We shouldn't move the eggs or the dragons before we know how the biology of this works. You might stop Gweeb's egg from hatching. We should let nature take its course.'

'We can't leave Gweeb down here in the cave all night,' said Mari.

'You'll have to leave her for longer than that,' said

Gareth. 'Think about it – she might have to incubate that egg for weeks.'

'And we literally have seconds now,' said Rhian. 'Come on, everyone. Go now, think later.'

Mari put Gweeb back down on her egg, and immediately felt the reptile relax.

'Come *on*, Mari!'

The others were nearly through the chicken wire now, training their torches on Mari like searchlights.

Mari stood there, and Gweeb gazed up at her, eyes wider than ever. Mari's head knew that leaving Gweeb here was the right thing to do – the scientist in her told her that – but in her heart it felt all wrong. Stripe landed on the ground next to Gweeb.

'OK, but you'd better look after her, Stripe,' said Mari.

And, with one last look over her shoulder, she was off.

They were all silent until they reached home and were sitting around the kitchen table.

'So, two dragons we can hide. But a whole flock?'

Dylan scratched his head.

'There are the danger signs, right?' said Rhian. 'And half the time the cave will be cut off by the tide.'

'So that keeps out the tourists and the dog walkers,' said Mari. 'But does it keep out nosy parkers like Petra Lunk?'

'That cave has been empty and dangerous for months,' said Dylan. 'There's no reason for her to go inside. Unless she gets suspicious.'

'But she *is* suspicious,' replied Mari, remembering how Petra had stared after them the last time they were down on the beach. 'I think she might have seen the dragons on the windscreen wipers. All it takes is for her to spot one dragon flying out to get food for his mate, and it'll lead her straight back to the nesting ground.'

'Can we feed them ourselves?' asked Dylan. 'That way they wouldn't have to leave. And we could guard the entrance to the cave, just to make sure.'

'We could,' said Mari, 'but that's going to attract attention.'

'You need a cover story,' said Rhian. 'A reason to be down there.'

'Hunting for fossils?' ventured Dylan.

'In exactly the same place? All day, every day?' said Mari. 'I don't think it adds up.'

They all scratched their heads and looked around the room, as if the answer to the problem lay hidden in the pictures on the walls. But then again, maybe it did. Mari's eyes came to rest on a decorative etching of a turbot that Gareth had brought with him when they moved in.

'Do you have a spare fishing rod, Gareth?' she asked.

A slow smile spread across Gareth's face. 'You mean, do I have a five-ounce beachcaster to catch fish right off the beach?'

It was Mari's turn to smile now. 'All we have to do is park ourselves by the cave with our fishing gear, and we have the perfect reason to sit in the same place for hours, and keep bringing down big boxes of worms – to use as "bait". Whenever the coast is clear, we can go back into the cave and replenish the dragons' food supply.'

Rhian put a proud hand on Mari's shoulder. It seemed like a pretty smart plan.

'But what if someone still tries to get inside the cave?' asked Dylan. 'What could we do to stop them?'

'If the worst comes to the worst,' said Mari, 'we go to the lifeguards and tell them. They're supposed to stop people doing dangerous things, after all.'

'Can you help us, Dad?' asked Dylan.

'I can get you started – with the fishing, that is – but Mari's mum and I have jobs to do. We can't be down the beach all day. I'm sorry.'

Dylan nodded.

'It might not take that long for the eggs to hatch,' said Rhian hopefully. 'I'm sure you two will be all right by yourselves. The cave didn't look too unstable inside, but I don't want you going in there any more than you have to.'

'Much safer learning to fish!' added Gareth with a snort.

Mari and Dylan exchanged a slightly concerned look. Maybe it wasn't a perfect plan, but it was the best they had.

So it had to work.

Mari turned her head restlessly on the pillow, her mind buzzing with everything that had happened that day. She looked across at the spot under the lamp on her desk where Gweeb would normally bask during the night, and felt the wrench of her not being there. She imagined the tiny dragon down in that cold, dark cave, the sound of the waves crashing against the rocks outside. She shivered at the mere thought of it. How was she going to sleep tonight?

She slipped out of bed and down the landing. Maybe Dylan was feeling the same way . . . She knocked on his door. There was a grunt that seemed to mean she could come in.

She opened the door to find him not in bed but still fully dressed, sitting on a chair with a battered old photo in his hand – the picture of his mum.

'Are you OK, Dylan?'

'Yep.'

'Need some company?'

'Nope.'

Mari nodded. She lingered just a second to see if he might change his mind, but he didn't. It wasn't fair to force it, even if she really wanted to be with someone right now. She backed out of his room and returned to her own. A moment later there was a knock at her door. But it wasn't Dylan; it was her mum standing silhouetted in the doorway.

'Can I come in?' she asked. Mari smiled a 'yes'. Rhian crouched down by the bed. 'It must be strange not having her here with you tonight.'

How did mums know this kind of stuff without being told? However Rhian's mind-reading trick worked, Mari was glad of it tonight. She reached out and pulled her mum into a hug.

'Why do things have to change all the time, Mum?' she asked as she snuggled deep into her mother's fleece.

'Animals grow up fast,' said Rhian. 'Gweeb was never going to be able to stay here forever.'

Mari swallowed hard. Maybe she knew that too, deep down. But it didn't make it any easier.

'And what about us?' she said, thinking out loud. 'Why did we have to change? I don't think Dylan wants a new family, and sometimes I know how he feels. We were OK how we were before, weren't we?'

Mari could feel her mum squeeze her that little bit harder.

'I liked it too, *cariad*,' Rhian replied. 'But you can't hold on to the past too tightly. Or it'll hold you back from the future.'

Chapter 10

'OK, this is your tripod. You rest your rod here while you wait for a bite.'

Gareth was trying to sound authoritative while he set up their fishing spot a safe distance from the cave, but he kept getting tangled up in the gear as if wrestling an unruly deckchair. Mari was trying not to laugh but Dylan seemed glum.

'And then, in here, you have your disgorger, for getting the hooks out of the fish's mouth.' Gareth snapped a pair of long-nosed pliers open and shut to demonstrate.

'We're not *actually* going to catch fish, are we?' asked Mari, suddenly attentive as she eyed the vicious-looking hook that Gareth had just pulled out of a little plastic bag. 'We just have to look like we are.'

'Don't worry,' he said. 'Most of the time you go fishing you don't catch anything. But if you're going to be spending all this time down here, you might as well try.'

Mari still wasn't convinced. She was pretty sure her mind would be on other things.

A nearby dog walker finally disappeared back up to the car park, leaving the beach empty.

'Shall I show you how to cast now?' asked Gareth.

'I'm going to see Gweeb first,' said Mari. 'I won't be long.'

She picked up a box of worms, scrambled up the rocks, pulled back the chicken wire, gave one last look left and right, and ducked down into the cave. Mari flicked on the torch she'd brought with her. She eyed the ceiling cautiously. She still didn't quite trust the rock to stay where it was meant to, but if it was all right for the dragons, it had to be all right for her. A couple of the creatures fluttered into the air, rudely awakened by the intrusion, but Mari wasn't worried about them. She only had eyes for the tiny dragon right at the front of the cave.

'Hello, little Gweebie,' she said, bending down.

The tiny red dragon raised her head to look up at Mari. It seemed like she was moving more slowly, and she gave a little shiver. Mari reached out and stroked her snout with a finger. 'Are you cold down here, Gweeb?' she asked.

Mari was worried. She couldn't take Gweeb home and put her under her desk lamp to warm her up, but she brought the torch close to the little body, in the hope that there might be a tiny bit of heat coming out.

'I brought you all something to eat,' said Mari, remembering the box. She scattered the worms liberally around the cave, and watched, delighted, as the dragons leaped on them like a flock of seagulls on a discarded bag of chips. Even more reassuring was the fact that she could see the boy dragons taking the worms to feed to their mates, who wouldn't leave their eggs, even for a moment. Stripe swooped down with a pair of worms in his mouth but Mari fed Gweeb herself. She felt it was the least she could do.

'I have to be getting back,' she said, nervous that getting out of the cave might be as suspicious as getting in if someone had appeared on the beach in the meantime. 'I'll be back when I can.'

Gweeb stretched out her tail as if she understood, curling it around Mari's little finger. Mari felt as warmed inside as if she were lying under her desk lamp herself.

Back down by the waves, Gareth was gone but Dylan was waiting.

'Now what?' he said moodily.

'We wait,' she replied.

'It's a long time to just wait,' said Dylan, after about fifteen minutes had passed.

'We could fish . . .'

Dylan laughed shortly.

'What's so funny?' asked Mari.

'What's the point?'

'What do you mean?'

'I mean, you sit around all day waiting for a fish to bite on your hook. You haul him out of the sea, take a look at him, then you throw him back in. What's the point? Why not just let the poor fish keep swimming around in the first place?'

'Lots of people seem to enjoy it –'

'Wrenching some little creature away from his family, away from everything he knows, just so they can say they did it? It's a pointless waste of everyone's time.'

Mari knew that Dylan was talking about more than fishing now, but didn't know how to talk to him about it. Didn't know if he even *wanted* to talk about it. So they just sat in awkward silence.

After a moment Dylan got up. 'I'm going for a walk. I don't know how long I'll be.'

Mari nodded. Maybe it was better to let him go and be by himself when he was feeling like this. She watched him crunch away across the stony beach, up on to the clifftops and out of sight.

She tried to make herself comfortable. What exactly was she going to do now? She picked up the rod from its tripod, but she had no idea how to cast, and wished now she'd waited for Gareth to show her. Maybe she could just go back into the cave . . .

But before she could move Mari spotted someone sitting a little way along the beach. It was a girl with blue hair. A little jolt of concern shot through her – the girl wasn't far from the cave – but then Mari realized it was Ffion Jenkins.

Ffion looked up and her eyes met Mari's. They nodded a greeting to one another, but no more needed to be said. Mari even felt a bit sorry for Ffion. Her popularity had never recovered from the chorus of mickey-taking after she claimed to have found a baby dragon. At their new secondary school, Ffion was the loner, just like Mari had been at primary school.

She seemed to spend more time with her collection of crystals than she did with other people.

Mari turned back round. The beach was filling up now. Mums and dads were nestling into sheltered nooks, colourful towels claiming their territory like the flags of explorers, their children already sifting through rock pools – tiny prospectors panning for gold. Mari thought for a second how simple it would be to have a family like that. Two parents, happy together, everyone playing on the beach. But she hadn't grown up with that, and neither had Dylan. And as the kids pulled a tiny crab out of the pool and shrieked with delight, she wondered for a moment how it might have felt if she had.

But then something wrenched her out of her daydream. Or rather some*one*. A man wearing a familiar leather flying jacket was striding along the beach, arguing with the woman walking next to him. The man was someone she knew only too well. Someone she'd hoped never to see again.

Dr Griff Griffiths.

Chapter 11

Mari could hardly move. Why was Griff back? He couldn't know about the dragons, could he? Had he seen her? She suddenly felt very exposed, alone in the middle of the beach.

They were getting closer now. Any minute one of them could spot her. Mari closed her eyes in the vain hope that, if she couldn't see them, they couldn't see –

'Mari Jones?'

Mari opened her eyes.

'Well I never,' said Griff, making his way across the rocks towards her. 'Fancy seeing you down here, eh? After all this time, the first person we see when we get back to Llanwerydd . . . is you.'

'You shouldn't be here, Griff,' said the woman with him. It was Nita, his girlfriend. 'You're meant to stay at least a hundred metres away from her.'

'Nita didn't want us to come back, you see,' he said. 'She says that Petra Lunk is a fruitcake. That when Petra called to say she'd seen Mari Jones and her family with something very *unusual*, it didn't really mean anything. She says we should forget all about the "D-words" and just get on with our new, rather unsatisfactory lives. Isn't that right, Nita?'

Nita cast her eyes to the ground. 'Griff,' she said quietly, 'it wasn't just me. That's what the judge said too.'

'So, have you been acting suspiciously, Mari? What do you think could have given our friend Petra this idea? Is there a *reason*?'

Mari shook her head.

'You're scaring her, Griff,' Nita cut in.

'Oh, it takes a lot more than this to scare Mari Jones,' he said. 'She's faced collapsing cliffs and swirling seas, haven't you, Mari? I'd like to think sharing that experience bonded us. Which is why it's all the more . . . upsetting that you COMPLETELY RUINED MY CAREER!'

'Mari!' came a shout from further up the beach.

But Griff's eyes didn't leave Mari for a second. He slipped a canvas bag off his shoulder and thrust it in her face.

'Would you like a Dr Griff's Dinosaur Hunting Kit? The kids used to kill for these.' He rooted around inside, and started yanking out the contents. 'Look, it's got a little hammer, and some little goggles, and even a shiny little rose-quartz key ring.'

The key ring clattered on to the rocks below and lay glinting in the sunshine.

'Griff . . .' said Nita, trying to calm him down.

Mari shook her head again.

'Are you sure, Mari? I've got twenty more in the car. Do you know why? Because now I CAN'T GIVE THEM AWAY!'

'Mari!'

It was a breathless Geraint Sharma, wearing a bright yellow T-shirt and red shorts, picking his way hastily over the rocks in his flip-flops.

'Is everything OK here?' he asked in his deepest voice, before turning to Griff. 'Please don't litter the beach, sir.'

Geraint bent down and handed Griff the fallen key ring.

Griff burst out laughing. 'Are you a *lifeguard*?' he asked, looking Geraint up and down.

'I'm in Lifeguard Support, sir.'

'Come on, Griff,' said Nita, putting a hand on Griff's shoulder. 'It's enough now.'

He glared at Mari for a second that felt like five minutes, before shrugging off Nita's hand.

'Of course, Nita, we mustn't upset *the authorities*,' he said as they started back up the beach. 'I'll be watching, Mari.'

And with that he was gone.

Geraint puffed out his chest like he had just single-handedly wrestled a crocodile to the ground. 'Are you OK, Mari?'

'I wasn't in trouble, Geraint,' she said, still a bit shaken. Well, she had been, a little bit. But she wasn't going to let on.

'I didn't know you liked fishing, Mari,' he said, taking in all the tackle next to her.

'I don't know yet either. Just trying it out for a few days.'

'That's cool. I'll just be back along the beach. You know, with the other lifeguards.'

'OK, great,' said Mari, wishing he would just leave her alone now.

'Maybe we could get that ice cream later? They've got mint choc chip.'

'Yes, maybe later.'

'OK, bye then!' Geraint walked off and Mari sighed deeply.

'Did I miss anything?' It was Dylan, who was finally back from his walk.

'No, not at all,' sighed Mari.

Guarding the dragons was going to be a lot tougher than she'd anticipated.

Chapter 12

The following day Mari and Dylan made sure to get down to the beach early. After the incident with Griff, they couldn't take any chances. There was a low tide first thing, and that meant they could get into the cave and check on Gweeb and the other dragons before any normal beach-goers turned up. And, of course, before the lifeguards arrived.

Nonetheless, they still made double-triple sure that the 'coast was clear' before peeling back the chicken wire and slipping into the cave. As ever, Gweeb was there, so near the front that Mari had to stop herself tripping over her. The dragon flapped her wings in welcome, eager for the treats that Mari might have brought with her.

'Here you go, dragons,' said Mari, scattering worms from a box she'd pulled out of her bag. 'And here's one for you and your little one, Gweeb.'

Gweeb gobbled the worm down in one go, immediately opening her mouth again, panting for more.

'Eating for two, I guess,' said Mari, plucking another one from the box.

'Hey, little guy,' said Dylan to Stripe as he flew up to land on Dylan's shoulder and head-butted him gently in the neck. 'Miss me?'

Mari lifted Gweeb's tail slightly to sneak a look at the egg underneath. 'And how is the even tinier dragon doing? I wonder.'

Dylan peered over to see for himself. 'It's not very big, is it?' he said.

'Well, no, it's an egg.'

He rolled his eyes. 'Yeah, but I mean, how does a dragon fit into that? It's much smaller than Gweeb, and she's the same size now as she was when she hatched.'

Mari pursed her lips. 'I was just thinking the egg looked bigger than I remembered.'

'Well, eggs don't normally get bigger after they're laid,' said Dylan, 'although these dragons aren't getting any smaller.'

'Nature will find a way,' said Mari, stroking Gweeb's snout. 'It always does.'

'Think I might go and check on Stripe again,' said Dylan. 'This fishing thing is really pretty dull.'

They'd been on the beach for an hour. Dylan was in a better mood today, but yesterday's encounter with Griff had left Mari's nerves slightly shredded.

'Someone could turn up at any minute,' she said. 'We have to be careful about going up there too much.'

'By "someone", you mean Griff?' said Dylan. 'I don't think he'll be back.'

'You weren't here when he came, Dylan. I don't think he's calmed down at all since he left.'

'Yeah, but he knows better than to come near you on purpose. He'd be breaking the law if he did.'

'I'm not sure if he cares about that.'

'You worry too much,' said Dylan. 'I'm going back up.'

He had pulled himself to his feet when they saw dust rising along the clifftop road that led to the car park above the beach. It was a camper van, and behind that a battered pickup pulling a rusty caravan with a Welsh flag flying proudly on top.

Mari and Dylan exchanged a look of concern. Griff was back, and this time Petra Lunk was with him.

All of a sudden Mari felt very small. How could two kids hold off determined adults all by themselves? There was a whole flock of dragons relying on them.

Dylan seemed to sense her anxiety. 'They don't know what we know, Mari. Remember that,' he said. 'We just stick to the story.'

'What's up, losers?'

Mari and Dylan spun round. Somehow, without them noticing, Ffion Jenkins had appeared.

'Morning, Ffion,' said Dylan, before pointing at his hair. 'Like the blue.'

Dylan had always been a lot more sympathetic towards Ffion than Mari had.

'Thanks.' Ffion nodded and walked past them, up towards the cave.

'Hang on,' said Mari, nervously looking over towards the car park and the approaching vehicles. 'You can't go up there.'

'Why not?'

'Because . . . it's dangerous,' said Mari. 'That's, er, where me and Dylan got trapped last year. It's still very unsafe.'

'Oh,' said Ffion, continuing to climb up the fallen rocks. 'I thought you were going to say because of the dragons.'

Chapter
13

'What did you say?' said Mari, not quite believing what she'd just heard.

Ffion stopped and turned. 'I said, I thought you didn't want me going up there because of the dragons.'

'You know about the dragons?' Dylan chimed in.

'Yes. Didn't you?' she replied.

'Yes!' said Mari and Dylan at the same time.

'That's good then,' said Ffion, turning back to keep climbing up to the cave.

Mari could see Griff getting out of his motor home in the car park, along with Petra and Gwyneth.

'You can't go in there now!' she cried, in a shouty kind of whisper.

'Why not?'

'Because *they* are coming!' Mari jabbed her finger in Griff's direction. He had started across the beach towards them. 'And *they* mustn't find out there are dragons in there.'

'Oh,' said Ffion. 'I see.'

She knew all about Griff. How obsessed he had become with the dragons and how badly that had turned out for him.

'OK, fine,' she said, coming back down.

'How's the fishing today, kids?' said Griff, clambering towards them. 'Get bored of fossil hunting, did you?'

'We like the beach,' said Mari firmly. 'What's your excuse?'

He made a big show of waving his nose in the air and sniffing loudly. 'Just taking in that sea breeze, Mari. Doesn't it smell great?'

'Not really.'

'Then you really need to work on your breathing,' said Griff, his arms spiralling in the air. 'Allow it to *circulate*.'

'Are we going to uncover *the truth* today then, Dr Griff?' asked Petra, approaching with Gwyneth by her side.

'Oh yes, absolutely, Petra. In fact, I have a good feeling about it today.'

'What are you doing here, Petra?' said Mari. 'With him?'

'Turns out, he might not be so crazy after all,' she said. 'I think maybe it was some *other* people doing the lying, and not him.'

Mari felt a bit queasy, but tried to remain calm. Petra could only have seen the dragons at a distance, in the dark and the rain. She couldn't be *certain*, surely?

'You don't really believe what he's been saying, do you, Petra?'

'Sherlock Holmes said that once you eliminate the impossible, whatever remains, however improbable, must be the truth. But, Mari,' said Petra, leaning closer to her, 'what happens when you've eliminated everything *but* the impossible?'

Mari laughed nervously.

'I just can't abide people not telling the truth, Mari,' Petra continued. Gwyneth barked loudly as if to agree. 'I know what I saw that night.'

'Where shall we begin our search, then, Petra?' Griff turned back to Mari. 'How about *our* cave? I haven't been back since that . . . incredible day.'

'No one has, Griff,' said Mari quickly. 'It's too dangerous.'

'It could collapse at any time,' Dylan pitched in.

'Oh, I'm sure we'll be all right if we just pop our heads inside,' said Griff. 'We know what we're looking for.'

'I don't know what you mean, Griff,' said Mari. 'There's nothing to find here. Your girlfriend's right, it's all in Petra's head.'

Petra glared at her.

'How sweet,' said Griff. 'Well, Nita's not here today. She has very important work at the university. And

I happen to believe Petra. Completely. So, if you don't mind, we have a lot to be getting on with.'

They pushed past Mari, Dylan and Ffion, heading in the direction of the cave, with Gwyneth straining at her leash. Mari was at a loss. There was a sick feeling in her throat. They were just at the foot of the rock pile when –

'Oi!'

A boy in red and yellow was bounding across the beach. It was Geraint again.

He stood in front of them, hands on hips, sneaking a quick glance at Mari to see if he was doing the right thing.

'Oh my goodness,' said Griff. 'It's Lifeguard Support again. Is someone in terrible danger?'

Geraint stood his ground. 'As long as you don't go up there, no,' he said, pointing to the cave.

'Or what?' said Griff.

'Or what what?' said Geraint. 'I don't follow.'

'He means,' said Petra, taking a pink-wellied step forward, 'if we go up there, what will you do about it?'

Geraint looked distinctly uncomfortable, and looked over at Mari in search of an answer. Behind Griff's back, Mari quickly made the sign of a phone with her hand against her cheek. She could see the cogs turning in Geraint's brain.

'If you do,' he began slowly, 'I'll have to . . . phone –' Mari nodded her encouragement – 'my dad.'

Mari's head dropped into her hands. Griff smiled and took a step forward.

'He's a police officer.'

Griff stopped in his tracks and Mari started smiling instead.

'This is a health-and-safety matter, sir,' continued Geraint, more confidently. 'My dad won't let the public put themselves in danger. And besides, I don't think you're supposed to be this close to Mari, are you, sir?'

Griff narrowed his eyes. Did he think Geraint was bluffing? 'You give Daddy a ring, then, Mr Lifeguard Support,' he said. 'Have you got a phone in those nice red shorts of yours?'

'We've got a landline back at the lifeguard hut.

Direct line to the emergency services,' replied Geraint. 'In case of . . . emergencies.'

Somewhere in the distance, a random siren wailed.

'Maybe one of my colleagues has already called him,' added Geraint, without missing a beat. 'Best stay safe, eh?'

Mari couldn't believe their good fortune. Griff wavered for a moment, then broke out into a fake grin again.

'Of course, young man. Very sensible advice. We shall steer well clear of the rockfall.' Then he stared straight at Mari. 'And this . . . girl.'

Mari did her best to stare straight back at him, but she could feel her legs wobbling underneath her.

'Come on, Petra,' said Griff. 'Let's start elsewhere.'

And, with that, they whisked off along the beach in the opposite direction.

Mari and Dylan let out explosive breaths.

'Is your dad really in the police?' Mari asked Geraint.

'Kind of,' he said. 'He's on the traffic side of things.

Well, the *parking* side of traffic things.'

'He's a traffic warden?' asked Dylan.

'He's a parking enforcement officer,' corrected Geraint.

'Well, thank you,' said Mari. 'That was some quick thinking.'

Geraint seemed to inflate a little with pride. 'Just doing my job,' he said, before pointing back up the beach. 'I'll be back at my station if you need me.'

'We'll be sure to throw up the Bat-Signal,' said Dylan.

Mari punched him on the arm.

'You've not been in that cave, have you, Mari?' asked Geraint.

She held his gaze for a moment, considering whether or not to tell him the truth. 'Of course not,' she replied. 'We just don't want to see anyone get hurt.'

Geraint nodded and picked his way back up the beach, his flip-flops slapping against the rocks.

Mari and Dylan turned to Ffion, and spoke at exactly the same time: 'How long have you known?'

Chapter 14

'I like to be on my own,' Ffion told them. 'And no one goes in that cave after most of it fell on your heads. So I bring my candles and my crystals and it's peaceful.'

'So when did the dragons arrive?' asked Dylan, hastily trying to get back to the point.

'A couple of weeks ago.'

'Why didn't you say anything?' asked Mari.

'After last time?' snorted Ffion. 'I'm not Griff. I've learned *my* lesson. Tell people you've found dragons and everyone thinks you're crazy.'

Mari felt a little pang of sympathy for her.

'Anyway,' continued Ffion, 'they're beautiful creatures, aren't they? I like being with them.'

That was one thing that hadn't changed about Ffion since last year. She still loved animals with every fibre of her being.

'So you won't tell anyone about this?' asked Mari.

'I haven't so far,' she replied. 'Why would I start now?'

'And you'll help us stop Griff finding out about them?'

'Sure, why not?'

'The keepers of the secret,' said Dylan, spitting into his hand and holding it out to Ffion.

She looked down at his hand and then up at him, trying not to laugh. She took his hand without being able to look him in the eye. Mari put her hand on top of theirs.

'We three,' Dylan continued, '*sworn protectors* will henceforth be known as . . . the Order of the Dragon.'

Ffion spluttered out a giggle.

'We five,' corrected Mari. 'If you include my mum and your dad.'

'Fair enough,' said Dylan.

'Right,' said Mari. 'We need to have a better plan. Because Griff will be back.'

'When Geraint isn't around to scare him off,' added Dylan sarcastically.

'If I was him, I'd come tonight,' said Ffion. 'At the next low tide.'

Mari had been worrying about the same thing. They couldn't stay here all night.

'When the tide comes back in to cut off the cove, we need to get home and talk to my mum and your dad,' she said.

'Can you make it back here tonight, Ffion?' asked Dylan.

'I don't know,' she replied. 'I'll do my best.'

Mari nodded. But for the time being they had a job to do. They sat back down next to the fishing gear, and settled in for another couple of hours' dragon guarding.

'Sandwich?' said Mari, offering a small tub to Ffion. 'They're hummus.'

Ffion smiled.

'You should really have spat on your hands too, you know, Mari,' said Dylan. 'To make the Order of the Dragon official.'

Mari and Ffion both pushed him at the same time, and he fell back into a box of fresh bait worms.

'Urgh!' he said.

'Exactly,' they said.

'You're not going down there on your own tonight,' said Rhian. 'And that's final.'

'But –'

'But nothing,' she said firmly. 'It's not safe. They're determined people. And they've got an enormous dog. Where are you going to sleep? How are you going to stop them if they really want to get into that cave?'

Mari looked over at Dylan for support, but she knew her mum was right. Three kids versus two grown adults and a bulldog were not great odds.

'What if I take them both in the car?' said Gareth from the doorway. He had just come back from his shift at the surgery. 'We can put the seats down and roll out some sleeping bags in the back. We can pretend we're night fishing.'

'I still don't see how that stops Griff,' replied Rhian. 'Especially when the lifeguards are off duty.'

Mari slumped. Her mum was right, again.

'Can we not bring the dragons back here?' asked Dylan. 'Put them in one of the barns?'

'I really don't think you should move them,' said Gareth. 'It could be dangerous for the eggs. And it wouldn't be easy either. Lots of dragons equals lots of chances to get found out.'

Mari stared out of the kitchen window at the dragon aviary they had built, and wished Gweeb and Stripe were still inside it. It was all so much simpler before.

Then a thought crept up and tapped her lightly on the shoulder.

'Gareth,' she said, 'could you build a stronger fence across the mouth of the cave? One we could lock so that only we can get in? So we could make the whole cave into –'

'An aviary,' he said, nodding. 'Smart thinking!'

He paced around the kitchen as he worked the idea through in his head.

'It couldn't be chicken wire; that's too easy to cut,' he pondered. 'It would need to be stronger, like railings.'

'What about the iron gate from your dad's old vegetable garden, Mari?' asked Rhian.

She and Mari exchanged a look. Mari's dad wasn't a popular topic of conversation since her mum had told her how he'd abandoned them when Mari was little. Before that, Mari had always idolized her dad and treasured anything that belonged to him. But things were different now.

'Good idea,' she said firmly. 'We don't need it any more.'

Her mum gave her an encouraging smile.

'OK,' said Gareth. 'But we need something solid to fix it to.'

'There should be some cement in the barn,' said Rhian. 'Could you block up part of the cave mouth with the stones, and fix the gate to them?'

'I should think so,' said Gareth. 'But we'll have to be quick. If they find us doing it . . .'

They sprang into action, but by the time Mari, Dylan and Gareth were back out in the car with a boot full of a gate, cement and tools, it was almost nine o'clock and getting dark. Mari looked nervously at the clock on the dashboard. Low tide wasn't until midnight, but the sea would already have retreated enough for people to go into the cove if they didn't mind getting their feet wet. She just hoped they weren't too late.

As they turned on to the lane down to the beach, Mari's heart skipped a beat. Coming in the other direction was Griff and Nita's camper van.

'They're going away from the beach – maybe they're giving up,' said Dylan hopefully. But even he didn't seem to believe it.

As they passed each other on the narrow road, Mari caught sight of Griff in the driving seat. He looked down at her, raised an eyebrow, and with one hand on the steering wheel he made an 'OK' sign with the other.

Mari had no idea what that meant. But she knew they had to get to the cave as quickly as they possibly could.

As Gareth pulled into the car park, Mari didn't even wait for the car to stop before she flung open the door and jumped out.

'Hold your horses!'

But Mari wasn't listening: she was already dashing across the beach. Dylan was hot on her heels, but Mari, much more practised at skittering across the uneven rocks and boulders, even in the darkness, raced on ahead.

The tide was still far enough out – Griff would certainly have had time to get to the cave before they arrived. Mari cursed their lateness, and began to fear what they might find.

Please be there, Gweeb!

She didn't dare think of the alternative. It was too much to bear.

Mari clambered up the rockfall. Someone had been there ahead of them. The chicken wire had been rolled back, and there was now a hole more than large enough for a flock of dragons to get out – or a group of humans to get in.

Mari's anxiety was reaching fever pitch. She stooped into the cave, thrusting the torch in front of her to illuminate the space.

It was worse than she could possibly have imagined.

There was not a dragon to be seen. Anywhere.

Chapter
15

Mari was still in shock when Dylan joined her in the empty cave.

'Where . . . ? What . . . ?' His mouth was opening and closing like a goldfish's.

'She's gone,' said Mari quietly. 'He's taken them all.'

'He can't have. They must have escaped before he got here.'

But they both knew what must have happened.

'I guess we won't be needing the gate now, then,' said Gareth, arriving on the scene.

'*Gweeb!*' Mari cried, as if her little dragon might hear her, wherever she was. But her voice's echo around the cave was the only reply.

'What time do you call this?'

At once, three torch beams whipped round to see who was talking.

'Ffion!' cried Mari.

'I thought we said eight thirty,' she replied, clambering down into the cave from outside.

'Well, where have you been, then?' asked Dylan.

'I,' said Ffion, swinging a rucksack off her back and on to the floor of the cave, 'have been looking after these guys.'

She peeled back the zips, and out crawled a teeming mass of tiny red dragons, all slightly dazed from being crammed into their temporary home.

'Gweeb!' cried Mari as the last dragon out of the bag flew up on to her hand.

She raised Gweeb to her cheek, to feel the dragon's scales against her skin. Gweeb curled her tail around Mari's ear, and it made her giggle with glee.

'So, fortunately, *one* of us was early,' said Ffion, a dragon perched on her finger. 'And when I saw Griff arrive in the car park, I had just long enough to stuff the flock into my bag and get clear before he and Petra came into the cave.'

'So they have been inside?' said Mari. But before Ffion had a chance to reply, she suddenly realized something. 'The eggs!'

She wheeled round and threw a beam of light over the cave floor, crouching down to get a better look. The female dragons that had spilled out of the bag were already spreading out across the cave in search of their eggs. Gweeb leaped down from Mari's palm to go to hers. Hard though they were to make out in the torchlight, Mari began to see the tiny eggs scattered among the rocks where the dragons had left them. She breathed an enormous sigh of relief.

'They must have thought the cave was empty and failed to see the eggs!' cried Mari. 'You're a superstar, Ffion. An absolute superstar.'

She stood up to hug Ffion. Ffion cautiously returned the embrace, as if she wasn't sure if Mari meant it or not.

Mari pulled back and held her by the shoulders. 'Thank you,' she said.

'You're, er, welcome,' replied Ffion.

There was an awkward silence for a moment, then Mari noticed a dragon appear out of Ffion's pocket. It had the same ruby-red body and emerald-green eyes as Gweeb, but its wings were streaked with black and it was holding a little crystal of rose quartz in one of its claws.

'Oh, this is Garnet,' said Ffion.

'Garnet?'

'He's a little red magpie. Loves stealing my shiny things. So I named him after a gemstone.'

'Nice to meet you,' said Mari to the dragon. 'Now, where's my little Gweeb.'

She turned round, expecting to find Gweeb back on top of her egg, but instead she was flapping back and forth across the cave floor. The other dragons had all found their eggs and were settling down on top of them, their mates sitting protectively nearby, but Stripe was just as restless as Gweeb.

'Your egg's right here, Gweeb,' said Mari. 'It's the first one you see as you walk in . . .'

Her voice tailed off as her brain kicked into gear. Gweeb's egg had been right at the front of the cave. What if someone had walked in, hoping to see dragons, but had seen a curious-looking egg instead? Is that what Griff had done? So thrilled to have found something that might finally prove his story, could he have rushed out with it before even noticing the others? With a sickening jolt Mari realized he hadn't been making an 'OK' sign as he drove past; he had been holding up the tiny egg between his finger and thumb – she just hadn't seen it in the dark.

'Oh, Gweeb,' said Mari, realizing what this meant for her and Stripe. The only dragons in the flock without an egg.

Gweeb was looking up at Mari, her green eyes sparkling in the torchlight, as if to ask where her egg might be. It broke Mari's heart that she couldn't explain.

'I'm sorry, little one,' she said. 'I'm so sorry.'

'What's going on?' asked Dylan.

'Griff has Gweeb's egg,' said Mari. 'And we have to get it back.'

Chapter 16

Gareth's car careered down the narrow country lane, headlights washing the hedgerows as they passed. They were hoping against hope that Griff might have taken the egg back to Petra Lunk's caravan.

Gweeb lay forlornly on Mari's palm, the energy sucked out of her. Mari stroked the tiny head with her finger, trying to offer some sort of comfort for her loss. Stripe sat on Dylan's shoulder, distractedly butting his head against Dylan's neck.

As they pulled into the car park by the lighthouse café, there was only one vehicle in sight – a big pickup truck with a bulldog in the passenger seat. Petra!

'Wait here,' said Gareth, climbing out to speak to her.

Mari, Dylan and Ffion peeked out of the window, careful to keep the dragons out of sight.

'Where's Griff?' Gareth was asking.

'Making history!' shouted Petra through her window, revving her truck so that the wheels spun as she pulled away, with Gwyneth barking like crazy and Gareth left coughing in a cloud of dust.

'What do we do now?' asked Mari as he got back into the car, brushing the sprayed-up dirt off his trousers.

'We get this lady home before her parents start worrying,' he replied, pointing a finger at Ffion. 'Then we get you two back home before your mum starts worrying,' he said, pointing a finger at Mari and then looking at Dylan. 'And then I'm going back to the beach to cement in that gate across the cave mouth, so it'll have dried by the next low tide. We can't take any chances on Griff coming back to find out what laid that egg he's got.'

Mari nodded, reassured. Gweeb's tail was curled limply around her little finger and she had dropped off to sleep. Her little dragon friend suddenly felt even smaller, even more fragile than usual. Mari knew that, above all else, she had to reunite Gweeb with her egg. But how?

The next day, Friday, Mari and Dylan returned to the beach early to check on the dragons and Gareth's handiwork. Mari would normally have been concerned about Gweeb trying to escape when they were away from the house, but today the dragon was just curled up in her shirt pocket, not moving at all. Every now and then Mari would give Gweeb a little nudge just to make sure she was all right, and the dragon would slowly stretch and curl round in the opposite direction.

When they got up to the cave, they saw what a good job Gareth had made of sealing it off. He'd piled up rocks on either side, cementing them in so they both supported the roof of the cave and braced the padlocked gate that he'd placed in the middle. It was dawn by the time he'd got home, yawning and covered in spatters of dried cement.

Mari was just about to get out the keys that Gareth had given her when she heard someone scrambling up the rocks behind them. She turned to see the familiar yellow-and-red of the Llanwerydd lifeguards. And Llanwerydd Lifeguard Support.

'I just saw the gate this morning,' said Geraint. 'It just *appeared* overnight.'

'I guess it must be the council,' said Dylan. 'Making sure it's safe.'

'Oh,' he said. 'Probably right, I suppose.'

Mari had feared that Geraint would be suspicious of a padlocked gate across the mouth of a dangerous cave, but as usual he had other things on his mind.

'I've brought my walkie-talkies,' he said, pulling them out of a shoulder bag. 'So you can call me at the station if there's anything suspicious going on down here. Don't suppose we need them now, do we?'

'I don't suppose we –' Dylan began.

'That's very thoughtful of you,' Mari cut in. 'Just because it's all locked up doesn't mean someone determined isn't going to try and get in. We should absolutely keep a careful watch.'

'Stay vigilant!' said Geraint proudly. 'That's what we lifeguards do.' (Dylan rolled his eyes.) 'Maybe we could go for a walk down the beach later, so I can show you how to use the walkie-talkies.'

'I think they work best if you go a long way in that direction,' said Dylan, pointing down the beach one way, before turning to point in the opposite direction. 'And we go a long way in that.'

'Why don't you look after them for now though, Geraint,' said Mari. 'Because you're nice and close if we need to get hold of you.'

'OK,' said Geraint, looking a little forlorn. 'I'll just be over there, then.'

He wandered back to his station. Mari and Dylan flopped down on to the rock. They clearly weren't going to get back into the cave right now. Mari peered into her shirt pocket. Gweeb was still listless and drowsy, and she seemed to be getting worse.

'I think she's pining for her egg,' said Mari.

'Pining?' asked Dylan.

'Feeling its loss. I think it might be making her ill. We have to get it back as soon as we possibly can.'

'Families should be together,' said Dylan, gazing out at some children shrieking with laughter as they ran away from the splashing waves.

Mari felt a lump in her throat, for both Gweeb and Dylan.

'But at least we have the chance to reunite these two, right?' he continued.

'Yes. Yes, we do.'

'So, where would Griff take that egg then? Back to the Brecon Beacons?'

Mari shook her head. 'No, he wants to show it off to the world. To prove he was right. Not hide away again.'

'So he'd take it somewhere to study it? To gather the evidence he needs?'

'Yes, but he lost his job at the university, so where would he do that?'

Dylan picked up a pebble and sent it skittering across the rocks in front of them. 'Hang on,' he said. 'Why did Griff say Nita wasn't with them on the beach last time?'

A big smile spread across both their faces.

'She was working *at the university*,' said Mari. 'It must be Cardiff University, mustn't it?'

But Dylan didn't reply. He was already up and running.

Chapter 17

There was no time to go home first. They ran straight to Llanwerydd station and jumped on the first train into Cardiff. They needed to be sure about where Griff and Nita had gone so that they could plan a rescue.

Mari stroked Gweeb through her pocket, but it didn't seem to be doing much good. The little dragon lay still and unresponsive. Dylan still had Stripe in his pocket so, when they could be sure no one was looking, they pulled down the tray on the back of the seat in front, and placed both dragons on it. Stripe crept over and twined his tail around Gweeb's. It seemed to bring a little bit of light back into her eyes. But it didn't stop Mari from worrying about her.

The Cardiff University campus was enormous, and thronging with students. As they stood outside the gates, it was a daunting sight.

'Excuse me.' Mari tried to get the attention of a passing girl. 'Excuse . . . ?'

It was lunchtime now, and everyone seemed to have somewhere they needed to be. Finally a tired-looking woman wearing a fluorescent jacket spotted them and wandered over.

'You two lost?' She looked slightly suspicious.

'We're looking for . . .' Dylan began. They hadn't worked out what their excuse was for being here.

'Our sister,' said Mari, thinking quickly. 'She studies fossils.'

'OK,' replied the woman. 'You want the School of Earth and Ocean Sciences.' She pointed at a building behind her. Following her finger, they could see not only the building, but also a familiar-looking camper van in the middle of the car park.

'That's fantastic.' Mari grinned.

The security guard raised her eyebrows wearily. 'Oh yes, amazing, isn't it?'

'Thank you!' yelled Dylan as they ran across the car park towards Griff and Nita's camper van.

The windows were too high up for them to peer in, so Dylan bent down on one knee and held out his hand to cradle Mari's foot. It was just enough to boost her up to see into the van. She scanned the interior. No sign of the egg. Just piles of clothes and empty takeaway food cartons strewn on the floor, papers and books stacked up the walls, and a tiny air vent on the ceiling.

'Nothing to –' Mari suddenly ducked down.

'What?' hissed Dylan.

She mouthed the word 'Griff!', pointing inside. After a second to get her breath back, she slowly straightened up again. Inside the van, she could see Griff gathering some journals together and stuffing them into a bag, before heading to the door on the far side. Just before he opened it, he grabbed something hanging on a hook by the entrance. It was the rose-quartz key ring he had thrust at Mari on the beach. He stuffed it into his pocket and threw open the door.

'Quiet,' whispered Mari, jumping down off Dylan's knee and pressing her back firmly against the side of the camper van. 'He's coming out!'

They both dropped to the ground and looked underneath the vehicle, just in time to see Griff's dusty boots hit the tarmac on the other side.

'He's going that way,' Dylan murmured, pointing.

They sneaked a look round the side of the van to see Griff buzzing himself into the building with a pass card. As soon as he was inside, they ran across the car park after him, but the door was firmly shut. They waited a few moments in case someone came out, but clearly no one in the School of Earth and Ocean Sciences needed to eat lunch. There was a panel to the left of the door with a bewildering selection of buzzers. Dylan started pushing the buttons randomly.

'Dylan!'

'What?'

A cacophony of 'Hello', 'Yes?', 'Reception!' came back at the same time.

Mari shot Dylan a disapproving look, as if to say 'Now what?'

'Er, delivery?' he said into the speaker.

There was a buzzing sound, and the door clicked open. Dylan shrugged sheepishly and pulled the door wide with a grin.

Finally inside, they wandered up and down staircases and corridors, on the lookout for anything that might give them a clue as to the whereabouts of Griff and the egg. But there was none. Just classrooms and labs, offices and storerooms, students and more students. They flopped down on to two blue sofas in the first-floor reception area, trying to work out their next move.

Mari was staring up at the ceiling, where the little red light on a lonely smoke detector was blinking on and off, when, suddenly, round a corner came Griff,

Nita and Petra Lunk, walking straight towards them. Mari grabbed two large leaflets on 'Geomicrobiology' (whatever that was) from a stand next to her and thrust one into Dylan's hands. They held them squarely in front of their faces as the adults went past.

'We need to wait for it to hatch,' Nita was saying.

'But we could get proof right now,' said Petra.

Griff turned from one to the other, thinking. 'We'll give it till after the weekend,' he said. 'A dragon is worth more alive than dead.'

'So what happens if it hasn't hatched by then?' asked Nita.

'We do what's necessary to prove I was right all along,' said Griff. 'We dissect it.'

'It's not right, Griff,' Nita said, shaking her head. 'How could you, of all people –'

'I've already looked like an idiot for far too long,' he said coldly.

Then they all disappeared round another corner.

Mari and Dylan put down their leaflets and looked at one another.

'*Dissect* it?' said Dylan. 'What does he mean?'

'He means that if Gweeb's egg doesn't hatch, they're going to crack it open to see what's inside,' said Mari furiously. She jumped up, grabbing him. 'Come on!'

'Where are we going?'

'To see where they went.'

They dashed round the corner, but the corridor was empty.

'They must have gone into one of the labs,' said Dylan.

The rooms here all had big windows on to the corridor, so they carefully peeked into each one. All the lab doors were locked, and they all had a small black panel to one side with a red light on it. You clearly needed an electronic pass to get in.

'Over here!' Dylan was jabbing his finger at a window.

Mari followed his finger right to the back of the room. It was Griff. He was holding a small clear box, though Mari couldn't see what was inside. He was putting it into something that looked like a small microwave.

'It's an egg incubator,' said Dylan. 'Dad's got one at the surgery.'

'Where are Nita and Petra?'

'Maybe they're in another lab.'

'Ow!' Mari exclaimed, putting her hand to her chest pocket.

It was Gweeb, thrashing around and catching Mari with one of her claws.

'What's got into you all of a sudden?'

The once-drowsy dragon seemed to have found a whole new lease of life. Mari had to clamp her hand over her pocket to stop Gweeb escaping.

'She must be able to feel that her egg is close,' said Dylan.

At that moment, a man in a lab coat came across the room, banged a green button next to the door and pushed it open. The kids froze.

'You kids lost?' he asked as he caught sight of them.

'We're looking for our big sister,' said Mari confidently. It had already worked once, after all.

'What's her name?'

'Nita?'

'Nita what? There are two Nitas.'

'Er . . .'

'Is it not the same surname as yours?'

'There you are!' came a shout from further down the corridor. 'I've been looking everywhere for you guys.'

Mari's heart sank. It was Nita.

'Ah,' said the man. 'You mean *that* Nita.'

'Don't worry, Dave,' said Nita, leading them away firmly. 'I've got this.'

Chapter 18

Nita bundled Mari and Dylan down the corridor, trying a few doors along the way, before one opened and she pushed them into the room. It was a security guard's office, full of CCTV screens showing all the goings-on inside and outside the building.

'You've got a cheek,' said Nita, her back to the door, blocking their escape. 'I'll give you that.'

'Where's the egg, Nita?' said Mari, feeling Gweeb straining inside her pocket.

'You're not getting it back,' she replied. 'It's too

important, and you know that. Griff hardly lets it out of his sight.'

'Are you going to dissect it?' said Mari, her voice quivering.

'Where did you hear that? Earwigging somewhere, were you? You ruined Griff's life, Mari. He'll do whatever it takes to get it back.'

'How does ending a life before it begins do that?'

Nita paused. Mari could tell that she'd hit a nerve. Maybe Nita didn't agree with Griff after all. Mari could feel the tears brimming now.

'Because if there's a dragon inside that egg, it proves that they exist, Mari,' replied Nita with a hint of regret. 'He's a good person deep down. But when bad things happen to good people –'

'You have to stop him, Nita!' Dylan cried.

'It's time you two went home,' she said, pulling open the door behind her.

As she grabbed Mari's jacket to haul her out of the room, something caught Mari's eye on one of the CCTV screens. It was a blurry image of Griff lifting the egg incubator into a cupboard on the wall. Then he locked the door with a key attached to the rose-quartz key ring, before stuffing it back into his pocket.

'I'm sorry,' said Nita as she marched Mari and Dylan down the stairs and out of the front door. 'I've told Griff we should wait for the egg to hatch naturally, but it's his egg and his decision.'

'It's *not* his egg!' replied Mari furiously. 'He's got no right!'

'Goodbye, Mari,' said Nita firmly. 'I really wouldn't come back here if I were you.'

And with that she shut the door behind them with an ominous click.

'What do we do now?' asked Dylan.

'We have a plan to hatch before the egg does,' said Mari. 'We've got till Monday.'

She looked inside her pocket. Gweeb was back to her languid, sickly self. Mari didn't dare think what would happen if they didn't succeed.

★

'There's no way you're breaking into the university and stealing that egg.'

Rhian's voice sounded final. They were all sitting around the kitchen table back at the farmhouse. Gweeb and Stripe were nestling quietly in an egg basket in the middle. 'It's too dangerous and, besides, it's illegal.'

'I agree with your mother,' said Gareth. 'You're kids, not bank robbers.'

'You're right. That's why *we're* not going to do it,' said Mari. '*You* are.'

The train ride home to Llanwerydd had given Mari and Dylan plenty of time to come up with a plan. Now they just had to convince their parents that it was a good one . . .

Mari went over to a small chalk board hanging by the fridge and rubbed it clean.

'Hey, that's our shopping list!' said Rhian.

Mari chalked a picture of an egg inside a box inside a box inside a box inside a box.

'The egg,' said Dylan, 'is inside an incubator, in a locked cupboard, in a room that you need a pass to get into, inside a building with a buzzer system, with an alarm that would go off if you broke in after hours.'

'Which is why we won't go in at night,' explained Mari.

'But in the daytime the building is full of people,' said Gareth. 'And Griff isn't going to leave the egg alone for long.'

'Exactly,' said Mari. 'So we'll have to make sure everyone is out of the building before you go in.'

Their parents looked slightly bewildered. Rhian took a big gulp of her tea.

'Dad,' said Dylan, 'you're going to pretend you're interested in being a student at the university.'

Gareth raised an eyebrow.

'You know, a *mature* student. And you're going to arrange to have a tour of the facilities.'

'Then, Mum,' said Mari, 'you and I will wait in the reception area for him.'

'But Griff knows us from when we rescued you all from the cave last year,' protested Rhian.

'We'll be in disguise,' replied Mari.

'Oh,' said Rhian, as if that explained everything.

'When Gareth's inside Griff's lab,' continued Mari, 'he's going to cause some kind of distraction and open the window a crack . . .'

'. . . then he and Rhian are going to head outside to wait in the getaway car,' said Dylan.

'The getaway car?' asked Gareth.

'I mean our car.'

'Then, when the time is right,' said Mari, 'I'll get Gweeb to breathe fire into the smoke detector in the reception area and set off the fire alarm, and I'll hide under the sofas until everyone is out of the way.'

'Outside, I'm going to send Stripe,' said Dylan, picking up his dragon and carrying him across the room, 'to fly in through the window, and open the door to the lab from the inside.'

'How's he going to do that?' asked Gareth.

'Because you don't need a pass to open the doors from the inside,' said Mari. 'You just hit a big green button.'

Dylan pretended to head-butt a button on the wall next to the kitchen door.

'Then I go in,' Mari went on, 'unlock the cupboard with Griff's key, put the egg into an insulated bag, and get down to the car as quickly as I can. What do you think?'

There was a stunned silence.

'How do you get Griff's key?' asked Gareth.

Mari and Dylan looked at one another. They hadn't quite worked that bit out yet.

'He keeps it on a hook by the door of his camper van,' said Mari, thinking out loud. 'So if we can get it early in the morning, before they go into the building . . .'

'You're going to break into the camper van while they're asleep?' asked Gareth, incredulous.

'Not us,' said Mari, the cogs in her brain whirring. 'We need something tiny that loves stealing shiny things, and could creep in through an air vent . . .'

Dylan smiled. He knew exactly what Mari was referring to.

'I don't like it,' said Rhian.

'Mum!' implored Mari.

'It's all so . . . risky.'

'What if it was *your* baby?'

'Now that's not fair, Mari,' replied her mum.

Gareth put a hand on Rhian's arm. 'I'm sorry, kids,' he said. 'I agree with Rhian: it's incredibly risky. The plan means that the dragons will be out in the open, where anyone could see them. And it relies on them being able to perform complex tasks they've never done before.'

Mari and Dylan looked downcast.

Then Gareth grinned. 'So we'll need to start training them as soon as we can!'

Chapter 19

'It's kind of a crazy plan, isn't it?' said Ffion when Mari and Dylan had finished explaining it to her, down on the beach. 'Breaking into the university? Setting off the fire alarm? And on top of that you want me to train Garnet to steal a key from right under Dr Griff's nose?'

Mari and Dylan nodded. 'You did say he likes taking shiny things,' Mari added hopefully.

'Well, personally, I like crazy,' said Ffion. 'But we don't have a lot of time.'

'Forty-eight hours,' said Mari, reaching into her pocket for a tiny padlock key attached to an identical rose-quartz key ring to the one Griff used. 'Thank goodness I still had my own Dr Griff's Dinosaur Hunting Kit from when I was a fan,' she added.

'Let's get started then,' said Ffion. 'You got the key for the padlock on the gate too?'

Mari pulled out another key from her pocket and handed it over.

'You don't leave anything to chance, do you?'

'I'm a scientist, Ffion,' replied Mari with her serious scientist face. 'We try to keep the variables to a minimum.'

Ffion raised an eyebrow. 'Right.'

'Let's see what Garnet can do,' said Mari, keen to get on with it.

Ffion nodded and they made their way up to the cave. Checking that the coast was clear, Ffion unlocked the heavy padlock, and they squeezed through the iron gate Gareth had cemented into place and pulled it closed behind them. A few small pieces of rock fell from the cave ceiling as it clanged shut. Mari winced. Even though she knew it was very unlikely she'd get caught in *another* cave collapse, she certainly wouldn't be coming here if it wasn't for the cave's precious contents.

'So how do we do this?' said Ffion as Garnet flew dutifully on to her hand.

'The key we need is on a ring, by a door, inside a camper van,' said Mari. 'But Garnet can only get into it through a vent in the roof.'

'Sounds simple enough,' said Ffion. 'Not too many variables there.'

'Are you joking?' asked Mari.

'Yes,' replied Ffion.

'Oh,' said Mari.

'Well, why don't you stand over there with the key, Dylan?' said Ffion, handing him the rose-quartz key ring.

'Why am I the hook?' he sighed.

'Oh, because you will be the absolute best at it.' Ffion patted him on the chest.

'Are you joking again?' asked Dylan.

'Yes,' she replied.

He rolled his eyes, picked his way over to the other side of the gloomy cave and stood with his back to the wall.

'Make your finger into a hook then, Dylan,' said Ffion with a smile. She seemed to be enjoying ordering him around.

He took a deep breath and held out the key on his curled index finger, the quartz glittering in the low light. Before Ffion could say anything, Garnet had sprung off her hand, darted across the cave and plucked the key ring from Dylan's finger. In seconds, he was back on Ffion's shoulder, admiring the pretty stone clutched in his tiny talons.

'Well,' said Ffion. 'That was easy.'

Mari breathed a sigh of relief. Maybe this plan would actually work.

'All we have to do now is train him to get in through the vent,' said Ffion. 'Piece of cake.'

'Are you joking?' said Mari and Dylan at the same time.

'Yes,' said Ffion. 'But leave it with me.'

'Thanks,' said Mari. 'We've got Stripe to train too.'

They made their way outside. Mari was relieved to be back in the sunshine.

'So, we'll meet back here, five a.m. Monday morning, and we'll head in together,' she said as they walked back up the beach together.

'What's that about five a.m. Monday morning?'

It was Geraint, who had appeared from his lifeguard station.

'Nothing, Geraint,' said Dylan.

'I was asking Mari,' he said.

'We're just going to Cardiff,' said Mari. 'Shopping.'

'Ah, I like getting there early to beat the crowds,' said Geraint. 'But I've got my shift.'

'We weren't inviting –' Dylan began.

'Oh, now that's a shame,' interrupted Mari. 'Next time, eh?'

They picked up their stuff and headed off the beach as Geraint trudged back to the lifeguard station.

★

'Do you have any ping-pong balls?' asked Dylan the next morning.

'This is a farmhouse, not a leisure centre,' replied Mari. 'Anyway, why do you want a ping-pong ball?'

'To make a green button,' said Dylan. 'For Stripe to practise head-butting.'

'I don't think we've got a ping-pong ball, but how about . . .' Mari rooted around in a cupboard, before triumphantly brandishing an . . . 'Eggbox?'

'I guess it'll have to do,' he said.

Half an hour later, Mari had cut out, painted and taped one of the cardboard egg 'cups' to her bedroom wall, next to the door. On the opposite side of the room, Dylan had opened a window just wide enough for a dragon to squeeze through. He held Stripe up and pointed to the 'button'.

'OK, little fella,' he said. 'This is the thing you have to push.' He held the dragon's snout close to the button, and made a butting motion with his own head. 'When you've flown through this window . . .'

He showed Stripe the window. 'Got it? There's a worm in it for you if you get it right.'

Mari held up a worm from a box she was holding. Stripe looked up at them both, as bemused as a dragon could look.

'Good,' said Dylan. 'Let's go downstairs and give it a try.'

A minute later, he was on the ground, looking up at Mari.

'Right, let him go!' she yelled.

Dylan thrust Stripe skywards, as if releasing a dove at a pop concert. Stripe flapped around momentarily before spotting an inquisitive robin and darting after it. Dylan put two fingers to his mouth and blew a shrill whistle. Stripe eventually circled back to his hand.

'Let's try that again, shall we?'

The next time, Stripe flew off to sit on an overhead cable instead. Mari fed a worm to Gweeb, who was curled up in her pocket.

'I'm not sure your boyfriend is up to this,' she said to her little dragon.

And then, as if he'd heard, Stripe flew straight from the cable in through the bedroom window and landed on Mari's shoulder.

Dylan punched the air with both fists. 'Never in doubt, Stripy!'

Mari looked down to see the two dragons' tails reaching for one another. She lifted Gweeb out of her pocket, stroked her snout, and placed them on the desk, giving both of them a worm.

'Getting there, Stripe,' she said. 'We're getting there.'

'Lunchtime!' yelled Rhian from downstairs.

'Dinnertime!' yelled Rhian out of the kitchen window.

The sun was throwing its golden light at Mari's bedroom window now, and Mari was trying to beckon Stripe through.

'We'll be there in a minute, Mum!'

'It's ready NOW!'

'He's definitely getting better,' Dylan shouted up.

Mari cocked her head to one side and raised an eyebrow. 'We've still got tomorrow, I suppose. I hope Ffion's getting on better than we are.'

But Mari was worried. They had never tried to get the dragons to do anything like this before. Herding sheep was one thing, but pushing buttons on cue was quite another. And Stripe was a particularly easily distracted kind of dragon. For the plan to work, every part of it had to go perfectly. She would never say it to Dylan, but Stripe was the weak link. If he didn't press the button, all their work would be for nothing.

That night, as she lay in bed with Gweeb curled up on her pillow as usual, Mari looked over at the weary dragon and feared the worst. The glint seemed to have gone out of her eyes, like a light that was being gradually dimmed. Her scales were starting to shed, and she seemed to be spending most of the day sleeping, as well as the night. They couldn't afford to fail. Mari wouldn't allow it.

She held out her little finger and let the dragon curl her tail limply around it.

'Goodnight, Gweeb,' she said quietly, hoping that the next day would bring them better luck.

Chapter 20

'How does this look?'

Mari turned to face Dylan, revealing a bright blonde wig and sunglasses.

'Like you're at a fancy-dress party?' replied Dylan. 'What's it for?'

'It's my disguise. For when we go back into the university.'

'I think you want something that is *less* likely to draw attention.'

'Oh,' said Mari, pulling off the wig.

'Let's get back to training,' said Dylan. 'The Order of the Dragon doesn't rest until the job is done.'

'Does the Order of the Dragon stop for breakfast?' said Rhian, poking her head round Mari's bedroom door. Dylan flushed red.

'It makes an exception for breakfast,' said Mari, covering his blushes.

But she couldn't help glancing over at Gweeb, curled up asleep under her desk lamp. They only had one more day to get things right and save her egg.

And the morning didn't go well.

Whoosh. In through the window went Stripe.

'No!' yelled Mari as he failed to find the button.

'Again!' yelled Dylan from the ground.

Whoosh!

'No!'

'Again!'

It was like that all the way up to lunch. And then afterwards . . .

Whoosh!

'No!'

'Again!'

All through the afternoon.

Until finally . . .

Whoosh!

'Yes!' yelled Mari.

Stripe had finally made it to the button, and given it a brief tap with his head, like the world's most nervous woodpecker.

Mari rushed to the window to celebrate.

Dylan thrust both his thumbs up to the early evening sun. 'Right,' he shouted. 'A few more to reinforce the behaviour!'

'I'd do more than a *few* more, if I were you.'

They both turned round and were surprised to see that Ffion was watching them.

'How long have you been there?' asked Dylan.

'Long enough to know you need more practice.'

'Well, are *you* ready?' asked Mari, slightly put out.

'Me and Garnet were ready about five hours ago, but I thought I'd give you a bit more time before I checked up.'

'You don't need to check up on us, thanks,' said Mari. 'We'll be ready.'

'If you say so.'

'I do. Say so.'

'Dinner's ready!' shouted Rhian out of the window, before noticing Ffion. 'There's room for an extra one . . .'

'Thanks, Mrs Jones,' said Ffion, 'but I can't stay.'

'We'll eat later, Mrs Jones,' said Dylan. 'We just need to do this . . . a few more times.'

Rhian raised both her eyebrows and shut the window. Mari raised hers too – how did Dylan get away with saying that to her mum and she didn't?

'OK,' said Ffion. 'Back to work!'

The next morning Mari hauled herself out of bed. She hadn't been able to sleep properly and she was glad when her bedside clock finally hit four and it was time to get up. Gweeb looked even more sickly than before, and Mari didn't know if she was more worried about the dragon's health or the heist's chances of success.

She pulled on a sweatshirt and looked in the mirror as she threw up the hood, drawing it tight around her face. She pushed some of her mum's old reading glasses on to her nose to complete the disguise. It wasn't brilliant, but it would have to do.

She lifted Gweeb up from her spot beneath the lamp. 'We're going to get your egg back for you, Gweeb,' she whispered. 'I promise.'

It was 4:45 a.m. when Gareth's car pulled up in the car park by the beach. He was wearing a ridiculous curly-haired wig and Rhian had on a pair of red, heart-shaped sunglasses. She winced as she manoeuvred her pregnant belly out of the vehicle.

'You OK, Mum?' said Mari. 'You can wait here while we get Ffion.'

'I'm fine, love,' replied Rhian. 'Good to get a bit of air for a second.'

'If we're quick,' said Mari, 'we can check on the other dragons. Ffion should be along in a minute.'

'Let's go,' said Dylan.

Up at the cave, he kept watch while Mari unlocked the padlock. They flicked on their torches and climbed down.

Mari had almost forgotten how beautiful it was down here. The tiny red flock glinted against the yellowed stone as their torch beams picked them out. And when Mari lifted Gweeb out of her pocket, they flapped their wings as if to welcome her back. Gweeb slowly raised her head to acknowledge them.

'Ow,' Dylan cried out all of a sudden. A small rock had dropped from the ceiling and cracked him on the head. 'I know people keep saying this cave might collapse again, but it won't really, will it?'

'We can't stop the process of erosion,' said Mari. 'It's been happening for millions of years.'

'That's reassuring,' he said.

'But around here, a part of the cliffs will only collapse perhaps once a year. Usually after rain, like last time. So it's statistically very unlikely to happen while we're inside.'

Mari hoped that would stop him worrying. Even if, on the inside, *she* still was. Dylan scattered some worms from a box on the ground, and the dragons that weren't incubating their eggs all crowded around to take the food back to their mates. Mari took a closer look at one of the nesting mothers. Her egg had grown again and was now almost the same size as the egg that Gweeb had hatched from. Mari hoped that the same thing was happening to Gweeb's egg, even if she wasn't there to care for it.

There was a sudden crunch of shoe on crumbling rock at the mouth of the cave. A shiver of panic shot through Mari.

'Anyone ready for a robbery?'

It was Ffion. Thankfully.

A dragon with black-streaked wings flew straight

to her as she ducked her head inside. It dived straight into her shirt pocket and pulled out the rose-quartz key ring that Ffion had been given to practise with.

'Good boy, Garnet,' she said.

Mari smiled.

'Let's do this,' said Ffion.

Gareth's car sped away from the beach, away from Llanwerydd, away from the things Mari knew, towards all the things she didn't. Her stomach felt like it was full of tiny flapping dragons. Dylan held out his hand and Mari was glad to grasp it. On her other side, Ffion did the same.

'Perfect,' said Gareth as he manoeuvred the car into a parking bay right outside the university.

'Right,' said Mari. 'Does everyone know what they're doing?'

Ffion and Dylan held out their dragons in their palms. Mari brought Gweeb out of her pocket to join them.

'The Order of the Dragon is ready,' said Dylan.

'What are *those*?'

Everyone whipped round at once to see whose voice it was.

From the boot of the car, Geraint smiled and waved a little sheepishly

'Hi, everyone,' he said.

Chapter 21

'Who are you?' demanded Gareth.

'What on earth are you doing in the back of our car?' asked Mari.

'Do your parents know where you are?' added Rhian.

'I'm Geraint Sharma,' replied Geraint. 'It was kind of a spontaneous thing, if I'm honest, Mrs Jones. And I thought maybe you might need me, Mari.'

Dylan spluttered. Mari put her head in her hands.

'But I didn't think you'd have, you know, dragons.'

'Yep,' said Mari. 'We've got dragons.'

'And you're, like, the Order of the Dragon?' asked Geraint.

'Well, I wouldn't . . .' Ffion began.

'We sort of are, yes,' said Dylan.

'And now you're part of it too,' said Mari.

Geraint puffed up with pride.

'Which means you are *sworn* to secrecy,' said Dylan. 'On pain of *death*.'

Mari shot him a look. Dylan shrugged.

'We need you to stay in the car,' said Mari. 'And be on the lookout for anything suspicious while we complete our mission.'

'What's your mission?'

'Dr Griff Griffiths has stolen my dragon's egg,' said Mari. 'And we're going to get it back.'

'Dr Griff Griffiths from the telly?' said Geraint.

Mari nodded.

'What a *scuzzball*! I didn't recognize him before. Well, it's a good job I came.'

Dylan rolled his eyes.

'Do I get a dragon?' added Geraint hopefully.

'No!' said everyone at once.

'Oh,' he said. 'OK.' He fumbled around in a backpack beside him. 'I brought the walkie-talkies!' He handed one to Mari.

Mari smiled politely. 'Thank you, Geraint. We have to go now.'

He saluted. 'I'll be right here, Mari. With my eyes peeled.'

'Positions, everyone,' she said. 'Phase One!'

It was time to put the plan into action.

They got out of the car, leaving Geraint on the back seat. Though it was far too early for anyone to be around, Mari pulled her hood tight around her face and slid her 'disguise specs' up the bridge of her nose. Then she put her hand to her heart, where she could feel Gweeb in her chest pocket. Dylan and Ffion checked their dragons too. They all exchanged a look, then nodded as they strode up to Griff and Nita's camper van. Without a word, Dylan bent down to boost Mari up so she could peer inside.

Through a crack in the curtains she could see Griff and Nita still sleeping and, over by the door, the rose-quartz key ring hanging on the hook. She gave Ffion a thumbs up.

Ffion held Garnet up, showing him the key on the hook. He seemed to strain towards it, as if he was going to burst through the glass.

'Up there, Garnet,' whispered Ffion, lifting him higher so he could see the air vent on top of the camper van. 'That's the way in. Just like we practised with the shoebox.'

Mari and Dylan exchanged a look that said, *Let's not ask.*

Garnet sprang out of Ffion's hands, and flew straight to the vent. The gang waited anxiously. They could no longer see what Garnet was doing. Mari's heart lurched as she watched Griff turn over in his sleep. And then, before she knew it, Garnet appeared inside, wriggling his way through the air vent.

Mari looked from the bed to Garnet, from Garnet to the bed. It was like one of those stories where the heroes have to steal something precious from a giant sleeping dragon. Except this time it was a dragon doing the stealing from a giant sleeping human.

Garnet flew over to the key, and expertly hooked it on to his claw. Ffion had certainly been an excellent teacher. Or at least Garnet was a far better student than Stripe.

Yawn!

Nita stretched and turned over in bed. Mari's eyes whipped to Garnet as he darted back up to the ceiling with the key in his grasp. Was Nita waking up? Had she seen him?

'*Down!*' she hissed, and everyone immediately crouched out of sight.

'Did you train him to get out again?' whispered Mari.

Ffion looked back at her nervously. Then, after a few worrying seconds, Garnet suddenly flitted off the roof and down on to Ffion's shoulder. She lifted the key out of his grip. Out of her pocket she pulled the matching key ring she'd used for practice, now with a small key that looked a lot like Griff's attached. Mari nodded to her, and Ffion placed the spare at the top of the steps that led up to the door of the camper van. If Griff woke up and discovered his key missing from the hook, he'd find it as soon as he stepped outside and assume he'd dropped it on the way in the night before.

'Are you sure you put the right one on the steps?' asked Mari when they got back to the car.

'Of course!' said Ffion, handing her the other key.

Mari turned it over in her fingers. 'OK. Even if they're suspicious, they shouldn't have time to test it before Gareth is in there on his tour. Let's sit tight until the building opens.'

'Well, that was easy!' said Geraint brightly from the back of the car.

Everyone turned round and gave him the same withering look.

At 9 a.m. sharp, Mari, Rhian and Gareth were buzzed into the main building, and headed up to the reception area on the next floor. They had been watching from the car, and there had been no movement from the camper van. Griff and Nita were obviously having a lie-in. Mari and Rhian sat down on the blue sofas and watched while Gareth announced his arrival to the receptionist. Rhian was shifting uneasily in her seat, and rubbing her belly.

'Are you OK, Mum?' asked Mari.

'Yes, love,' she said, but her smile wasn't as reassuring as Mari would have liked.

Gareth waved to them both as he wandered off on his tour. It would be about ten minutes before the tour reached Griff's lab. All they could do was wait. And hope that –

CSSSSH!

A burst of static erupted from Mari's pocket.

'THIS IS GERAINT CALLING MARI. OVER.'

Mari leaped up like a bee had got caught in her trousers, her hands desperately searching for the source of the noise as the receptionist looked over to see what the commotion was about. She grabbed the walkie-talkie and fumbled for the TALK switch, sliding down into her seat as if that might make her less conspicuous.

'Not now, Geraint!' she hissed in a loud whisper, before remembering she needed to say, 'Over.'

She flipped the walkie-talkie round to try and find the OFF switch.

Cssssh!

'Dr Griff Griffiths from the telly on his way to you now,' said Geraint at a more reasonable volume level. 'Over.'

'Thank you, Geraint. Over and out.' Mari twisted the volume knob even further down and slipped the device back into her pocket. She felt a sudden shiver of panic and glanced over at her mum. Was this really going to work? Rhian seemed to be thinking about something else, though. Her face was scrunched up like she was holding back a pain.

'Are you sure – ?' began Mari, before stopping in her tracks and yanking on the drawstring on her hoodie as tightly as possible. It was Griff and Nita.

She needn't have worried about being spotted though: Griff didn't even glance at who was sitting in reception. He made a beeline for his lab, with Nita trailing behind him. Then he seemed to remember that he didn't have a pass, and had to wait for Nita to buzz him in.

'Come on, come on,' he said impatiently. 'It might have hatched overnight.'

Nita swung the door open with a flourish, and made a sarcastic bowing gesture to usher him in.

'Go and see what he's up to,' said Rhian, through slightly gritted teeth.

At that moment, though, Gareth appeared at the other end of the corridor with the woman who was showing him round. 'Any questions?' she asked.

'Actually, I'd love to look in here,' said Gareth, pointing to Griff's lab. 'Check out the facilities, you see.'

'Of course,' said the woman, waving her pass at the door and buzzing them both inside.

Mari sneaked up to the door to see what was

unfolding inside. There were several students working at benches around the edges of the room. Gareth and the guide were standing to one side, talking. Mari couldn't hear what was being said, but as the woman was pointing at some complex-looking equipment, she saw Gareth pull something small out of his pocket and crack it open between his fingers. It was a stink bomb.

Mari watched people's hands reaching for their noses as the awful smell rippled around the room like a malodorous Mexican wave. Griff had been heading for the cupboard where the incubator was kept, but the scent had stopped him in his tracks. He looked over at Gareth, narrowing his eyes as if he knew him from somewhere. Which of course he did – Gareth had been piloting the boat when they plucked Griff out of the sea last year.

Mari tensed, but Gareth ignored Griff, wafting his hand over his nose as he apologized for being the source of the scent. Griff finally turned away as Gareth went over to a window. For a moment he struggled to open it and Mari's breath caught in her throat. Surely their plan couldn't fall at the first hurdle? She felt Gweeb wriggling in her pocket, as if she knew there was a problem. Then the window slid down, leaving a gap more than large enough for Stripe to fly through. Mari relaxed at last. She put her hand to her 'Gweeb pocket'.

'Now it's time for you to do your stuff,' she whispered to Gweeb, worried that Griff might already be opening the cupboard with the egg in it.

She hurried back to the reception area and, checking that no one was watching, reached into her bag and plucked out a worm. She watched as her little dragon slowly munched her way through it. Gweeb's energy levels were still incredibly low. Mari prayed that she would still be up to the job of breathing fire. Shielding the dragon from any prying eyes, Mari lifted her out of her pocket, jumped on to the sofa and raised her up towards the smoke alarm on the ceiling.

'Come on, Gweeb,' urged Mari. 'This is it.'

'Mari,' said Rhian.

'Just a minute, Mum!'

Gweeb opened her jaws and seemed to wheeze for a second, but no flames emerged. Mari began to panic. They had spent all that time training Stripe to fly in through a window, but hadn't given a second thought to Gweeb being able to breathe fire on cue.

'Mari –'

'Mum, not now. Come on, Gweeb!'

Still nothing.

'Mari, I need to go to the hospital.'

In shock, Mari looked down at her mum.

'I think the baby's coming. Right now!'

Chapter 22

'What's going on?' asked a worried Gareth as he finished the tour and came back to find them in reception.

'She says the baby's coming,' said Mari.

'What? But she's not due for another two months yet,' he said. 'Are you sure, Rhian?'

Rhian's look said more than words could have done. It was a look that said this was serious.

'Can you get back to the car?' he asked.

Rhian shook her head. 'Ambulance,' was all she could say.

Gareth nodded. 'OK, Rhi, don't worry. It's going to be all right.'

He pulled out his phone to call the ambulance, leaving Mari and her mum alone together for a moment.

'I'm coming with you, Mum,' said Mari, taking her mother's hand in hers.

Rhian shook her head again. 'Stay. You've got a job to do.'

'But this is more important.'

'I've got Gareth. Gweeb only has you.'

Mari could feel the panic rising up inside her. There were too many things to worry about all at the same time.

'Be as quick as you can,' said Rhian. 'Don't let Griff catch you. Then come and find us. You can walk to the hospital from here. Stay safe.'

Mari felt a little reassured. But only a little.

'Ambulance is on its way,' said Gareth, taking Rhian's other hand.

'Mari's staying,' she told him. 'To do what she has to.'

'OK,' said Gareth, reaching out for Mari's free hand with his so they formed a little circle.

Rhian was taking quick, shallow breaths. It looked like she was in pain, and that made Mari worry even more. Then she felt her mum's hand gripping hers, and Gareth's too, as if they were squeezing courage into her. Time seemed to slow down to a crawl as Mari finally made out a faint siren that drew reassuringly nearer and nearer.

Before long, Mari heard people running up the stairs, then the paramedics bursting into the hall.

'Sorry, love,' said one of the medical team. 'We're going to need some space.'

Mari let go of her mum's hand and stood back, feeling powerless.

'Griff!' said Gareth. 'Quick!'

Mari whipped round just in time to see Griff emerging from the lab to see what the commotion was. Before he spotted her, Mari rolled under the sofa to hide. She didn't think her heart could beat any more quickly, or any more strongly. She peered out across the floor in front of her, the black boots of the paramedics joined by Griff's hiking trainers.

'What's going on here?' Mari could hear Griff asking.

'Please stand back, sir,' replied one of the paramedics.

'Wait – I knew I recognized you,' he said. 'You're Mari's parents.'

'Now's not the time, Griff,' said Gareth.

Mari craned her neck to try and see more. Her eyes scanned up Griff's legs until she could see his hands hanging down and, tucked between his thumb and forefinger, the glint of a tiny key attached to a piece of rose quartz. Had he already tried to open the cupboard? Did he already know he had the wrong key? She felt in her pocket, and gripped the real one tightly. She just needed Griff out of the way so she could get inside.

As soon as his legs had disappeared and she could hear the paramedics moving off, Mari rolled out from beneath the sofa. The coast was clear – for the moment at least. She climbed back on to the cheap blue upholstery, and lifted Gweeb up to the smoke alarm once more.

'Come on, Gweeb,' she urged. 'Do it for my mum.'

Outside in the car park, Dylan and Ffion had been getting worried and impatient. Well, Dylan was getting worried, and Ffion was getting impatient. They had seen the lab window open ages ago, but they still hadn't heard the fire alarm.

'It shouldn't have taken this long,' said Dylan. 'Something must have gone wrong.'

In the distance, a siren began to wail.

'Did you hear that?' asked Dylan. 'Is that the fire alarm?'

'Fire engine, more like.'

The siren was getting closer, and louder.

'Something's definitely wrong,' said Dylan. 'I'm going back to the car to see if Geraint's heard anything.'

He had just set off when the siren that had been wailing in the distance was all of a sudden wailing right in front of them. An ambulance careered round the corner into the car park.

Dylan stood dumbstruck as a couple of paramedics piled out of the vehicle and ran into the main building.

'I should go in,' he said.

'Wait,' said Ffion, holding him back. 'We don't know who the ambulance is for. Let's ask Geraint first.'

But before they could take another step towards the car, Geraint was running at full pelt towards them.

'It's Mari's mum!' he puffed. 'She's having the baby!'

'She's what?' asked Ffion.

'But it's too early,' added Dylan with genuine concern.

'And Mari's hiding under the sofa in reception!'

'She's where?'

Dylan and Ffion exchanged a bewildered look.

'So what are we supposed to do now?'

'She said, "Stick to the plan!"' said Geraint.

'She said *what*?' replied Dylan.

'Here comes Rhian!' said Ffion, pointing to the main door.

Rhian was being wheeled out of the building by the paramedics, with Gareth on one side of her *and Griff on the other*.

'OK. We stick to the plan,' said Dylan. 'Griff is outside the building, that's all that matters. We have to stop him going back in. Ffion, you keep him busy so I can get Stripe to open the lab door for Mari.'

'What?'

'Now!'

Ffion gulped and ran towards the back of the ambulance to intercept Griff, who was hurrying alongside Rhian's wheelchair, demanding answers in a high-pitched voice.

'What are you doing here?' he was asking.

'I said, stand back, sir,' said a paramedic, trying to push him clear of the chair.

'Where's the girl? Where's Mari?' Griff was getting really agitated now.

'You're talking like a crazy person,' said Gareth. 'Keep away from her!'

'Let it go now, Griff,' said Nita, catching up with them. 'The woman is having a baby.'

'Shut up!' he cried, turning on her. 'Who knows what's really going on? They're liars, the Joneses, all of them!'

'Dr Griff Griffiths! From the telly?' cried Ffion. 'It is, isn't it?'

'Not now!' he yelled. 'I'm busy.'

'And we're busy too,' the paramedic told him, elbowing him aside.

'I'm trying to ask this woman a very important question!'

'That's enough, Griff!' said Nita, trying to pull him back.

'Get your hands off me, Nita!' he shouted, shaking her off.

Nita stood back and held both hands in the air in surrender.

'Can I have your autograph?' Ffion asked Griff, for maximum distracting effect. 'I'm a *huuuuge* fan.'

'Where. Is. Mari?' he bellowed at Rhian.

'At home!' said Gareth. 'Now leave us alone!'

The paramedics loaded Rhian into the ambulance; Gareth climbed up next to them and gave a thumbs up to Ffion that only she could see; then the doors slammed shut behind them.

Griff glared at Ffion, and whipped round to go back into the building – just as the fire alarm rang out across the car park.

'Argh!' he yelled in frustration. 'What *now*?' He started towards the door.

'You can't go back in during a fire alarm, Griff,' said Nita.

'I'm Dr Griff Griffiths and I will do what I want!'

He marched forward with Nita in tow. Ffion looked over at the door, where a burly security guard in a fluorescent jacket looked like he was going to make getting inside very tricky for Griff.

There was nothing more she could do, so she rushed back to Dylan, waiting beneath the open window to the lab.

As she approached, Ffion saw Stripe lift off from Dylan's hand and dart upward.

Dylan swallowed. 'It's up to him now.'

Chapter 23

The fire alarm was incredibly loud. It had given Mari a tremendous shock when Gweeb finally mustered a tiny flickering flame to set it off. She'd had to dive back under the sofa immediately to hide from all the people trooping past to get out of the building. Finally, when the building was empty, she had crawled out again, taking pains to shield the frail dragon from the noise.

Mari pressed her face up against the glass window to Griff's lab. She was peering through to the open window on the other side, waiting for the yellow-striped dragon to appear. Her own tiny, exhausted dragon sitting in her palm looked up at her expectantly. But now it was up to Stripe.

'Come on,' she muttered under her breath. Any moment, the alarm could stop and everyone would start trooping back in.

Her heart leaped as a tiny red shape appeared at the window opposite. Stripe bounced against the glass like a confused sparrow.

'Up! Up!' she urged, pointing with her finger, trying to show Stripe the gap above him.

He was much too far away to see what Mari was doing, of course. He dropped on to the window sill, distracted.

'No!' she yelled.

She felt panic rising again. She banged against the glass in the vain hope of getting his attention. Finally Stripe caught sight of her and Gweeb across the room. Instantly he flew up and through the open window, swooped across the lab and hit the green button next to the door with a perfectly weighted head-butt.

'Never in doubt!' cried Mari as she pulled the door open.

While Stripe was happily reunited with Gweeb, and given some worms as a reward, Mari rushed over to the window. Down on her right she could see Griff, Nita and Petra Lunk arguing with a fire marshal, and off to her left Dylan and Ffion were hiding behind a car. They caught sight of Mari and punched the air. She gave them a big thumbs up, but her smile faded rapidly as the alarm suddenly stopped ringing. Any second now the crowd would be let back into the building.

There was no time to waste. Mari rushed over to the cupboard that held the incubator. She pulled out Griff's key and jammed it into the padlock that held the door handles together, but the lock wouldn't budge. She rattled it around, but it seemed to make no difference. She tried again; still nothing. The egg was just centimetres away from her, but it might as well have been miles. Mari hit the door with her open palms in frustration.

And then, just when she thought there was nothing more she could do, Gweeb and Stripe landed on her outstretched arms. Gweeb was revitalized, clearly sensing how close her egg was. In unison, she and Stripe let loose two jets of flame at the padlock.

'It's no use,' said Mari. 'It's metal. It's too hard to melt.'

But then she realized that the jets weren't focused on the padlock. They were melting the plastic handles of the doors! In seconds, the padlock had dropped clean off and Mari was able to pull the doors wide open.

'Yes!' she cried as the incubator was finally revealed. 'You little geniuses!'

She quickly opened the incubator. Nestled inside was Gweeb's precious egg. Like the eggs in the cave, it had grown, and was now the very same size as the egg Gweeb herself had hatched from.

Gweeb immediately flew to embrace the egg like the long-lost child it was. Mari pulled a small insulated bag out of her rucksack, and slipped both dragon and egg inside. Stripe joined them, and Mari threw in a few worms for good measure before clipping it shut again.

She could already hear people coming back up the stairs. She ran to the door, and punched the green button to let herself out. She looked left to the stairs – there was no way she could go back that way; she looked right, to the other end of the corridor, where a narrow door was marked as an emergency exit. She ran full pelt to crash through the door and leave it swinging in her wake, just as Griff and the others rounded the corner . . . too late to stop her.

Down some concrete stairs and out through another door into the welcome fresh air, Mari practically fell into Dylan and Ffion's arms. Geraint hung back sheepishly, but they pulled him into the group hug.

'We did it,' was about all Mari could manage to say.

But they couldn't enjoy their victory a moment longer. By now Griff would know that the egg had gone: he would be out of the building any second in pursuit of the culprit.

'I need to go to the hospital,' said Mari.

'Then we're coming too,' said Ffion.

Half an hour later, the four kids were bunched up in the corner of a waiting room in the maternity ward. Mari sat in the middle with her rucksack and its precious cargo on her lap. A kindly nurse smiled over at them.

'I'm sure we'll have news soon,' she said. 'She's in really good hands.'

Mari knew that was true, but the relief of rescuing Gweeb's egg had now been completely overtaken by the worry about her mum and the baby. She could sense that Dylan was feeling it too. A premature birth was risky for both mother and child. But the nurse was right – Rhian was in the best place she could be, and all they could do was wait.

'What will Griff do now?' asked Ffion, interrupting Mari's train of thought.

And it was an unwelcome question, because Mari hadn't really considered what Griff might do if they got the egg back. He would naturally suspect that she had something to do with it. Maybe he was already waiting outside the farmhouse. Or would he go back to the beach? To the cave where all the other eggs lay hidden? She hoped that the padlock they'd put on the gate would keep him out, but there was no guarantee. She answered Ffion's question with a pained shrug.

'Can I see the egg?' asked Geraint eagerly, his mind on more exciting things. 'And the dragons?' he added with a whisper so the nurse couldn't hear.

Mari was happy to turn her attention to the good news story. And Geraint and his walkie-talkies had been unexpectedly helpful in the end.

'OK,' she said. 'Carefully now . . .'

She slowly unzipped her rucksack, and pulled back the sides to reveal the insulated bag within. Keeping it in the rucksack to shield it from prying eyes, she unclipped the clasps holding the little bag shut, and gently peeled back the top. Geraint leaned over to gaze in wonder at the scene – two tiny, sleeping red dragons, their tails curled around each other, their bodies curved round the egg to form a heart-shaped embrace.

Geraint reached in to touch the egg.

'What are you doing?' hissed Dylan.

He pulled back his hand immediately, like he'd scalded himself with boiling water. 'Sorry,' he said. 'I just didn't think it would be made of stone.'

'Made of stone?' asked Mari and Dylan in unison.

They both peered into the bag to take a closer look. In all the rush of stealing back the egg, Mari hadn't noticed that anything was different about it. But it was. Very different. She held out a shaking finger and pressed the tip against the cold surface of the egg.

There was no doubt about it. Gweeb's egg was no longer a fragile container of new life.

It had turned to solid rock.

Chapter 24

'It's OK, Mari,' said Dylan, putting his arm round her.

Mari was sobbing, great heaving sobs. All the desperate worry and stress of the day had come to this. Gweeb's egg turned to stone, Griff on the loose, her mum in hospital – and what about her baby sister? It didn't bear thinking about.

Ffion put her arm round Mari's other shoulder. 'It's not OK, Mari,' she said. 'No point in saying anything different. But we're going to stick right here with you. Till it's better.'

Mari turned to Ffion and wiped a tear off her cheek. She would never have believed last year that this girl would be her friend. But she couldn't be more grateful now.

'So that's one thing you don't have to worry about, isn't it?' added Ffion quietly.

'Mari!' came a shout from across the room. It was Gareth. In a trice he was kneeling down in front of them.

'Your mum's OK, Mari,' he said, before placing a hand on both her and Dylan. 'And so is your sister.'

Mari blew out a breath that she felt she had been holding in for hours. She laughed with the relief of it.

'Would you like to see them?' asked Gareth.

It only took two heartbeats for Mari to race across the ward and collapse into her mother's arms.

'It's all right, *cariad*,' said Rhian. 'Everything's all right.'

Eventually Mari raised her head, and saw that her mum's bed was next to a plastic incubator. And sheltered inside, among a web of tubes, was the tiniest baby she had ever seen.

'She arrived before we had a name ready for her,' said Rhian. 'But she's perfect.'

Mari pressed her nose up against the plastic, and lifted her hand so that her fingers could almost touch the tiny hand on the other side.

'Is she going to be OK, Mum?'

'Oh yes,' said Rhian. 'She's a fighter, like her big sister.'

Mari smiled.

'Did you manage to finish the job, Mari?' asked Rhian. 'The one we came to do?'

Mari's lip quivered. If only it was as simple as that.

Before she could answer, Gareth arrived with the others. Dylan joined Mari at the incubator, instantly fascinated.

'Hey, little sis,' he said softly.

'We should get going, I think,' said Ffion, meaning her and Geraint. 'My dad is probably wondering where I am.'

'I know,' said Gareth. 'I'll run you back.'

'It's OK, Mr Moss, you need to be here,' said Ffion. 'Me and Geraint can take the train.'

'If you're sure?'

Ffion nodded. 'And as soon as I get back, I'll check on the cave.'

'And if Griff and his gang try returning, I'll make sure they don't get in,' said Geraint. 'Lifeguard's honour,' he added with a little salute.

'Thank you,' Mari said to them both. 'For everything.'

'We're the Order of the Dragon, isn't it?' said Ffion with a wry smile.

'We'll meet you down there later,' said Mari. 'When the tide has turned.'

And, with a nod and a wave, Ffion and Geraint were gone.

'So,' said Rhian. 'Time to tell me and your sister all about what happened . . .'

Mari and Dylan spent the rest of the afternoon at the hospital. Rhian had fallen asleep for a few moments and Gareth had gone to get a cup of tea, leaving them alone together. They couldn't help staring at the baby in the incubator. It was like they were hypnotized by it.

'Things are different now, aren't they?' said Dylan.

'What do you mean?'

'I mean, we're a real family now.'

'We were before, Dylan.'

'Yeah, but now, with the baby . . . it's forever, isn't it?'

Mari could feel it too. Their family was tied together by this tiny person in a transparent box. Set in stone like Gweeb's egg.

'That's OK, though, isn't it?' asked Mari.

Dylan didn't speak for quite a while. Then, very quietly, he said: 'But I don't look like my little sister. And I don't look like you.'

Mari turned to him, confused.

'I mean, I look like my mum,' he explained. 'But she isn't here any more. And now, you're all the same, and I'm not.'

It had never occurred to Mari that this was how Dylan might feel. That he might even have been feeling like this ever since he moved in. And a great wave of understanding washed over her. She reached out to hold his dark-skinned hand in her light-skinned one. They stared at the baby for the longest moment before Mari finally broke the silence.

'I think we're all the same,' she said. 'In every way.'

He turned to her and smiled, a little tear forming in his eye, and squeezed her hand back.

When it was time to go, Mari hugged her mum goodbye – she and the baby would be staying in hospital for a few days – and asked Gareth to take them straight to the beach. Maybe there was something they could do for the other dragons that might somehow make her and Dylan feel better.

Sitting in the back seat of the car, she opened up her bag again, and Gweeb and Stripe both climbed out. Stripe darted to his usual perch on Dylan's shoulder, and Gweeb nestled into Mari's palm.

'I'm sorry, Gweeb,' she whispered.

But Gweeb, for her part, still seemed revitalized. Her scales were shining again, the depth of her colour had returned. And, perhaps most strange of all, she didn't seem to be concerned about the egg any more. She was happy to leave it where it lay, back in the insulated bag.

The car started bumping from side to side. They were back on the potholed lane down to the beach.

'Hide the dragons!' cried Gareth suddenly. 'It's Griff!'

Mari craned her neck round to see through the windscreen and, sure enough, there was Griff's camper van parked up next to Petra Lunk's pickup. Mari was instantly on full alert.

'Are we too late?' she asked in a bit of a panic. 'Maybe he's managed to get to the cave already. What if Geraint wasn't able to stop them?'

Mari didn't wait for anyone to answer her questions. The second the car was parked, she was out of the door and away, Gweeb safely tucked into her top pocket.

As she hurried across the stony beach, Mari could see that everything was *not* all right. There were groups of people gathered on the shoreline, but they weren't staring out to sea – they were all facing back towards the cliffs.

Mari was now full-blown frantic – what had happened? When she reached the assembled crowd, it became perfectly, horribly clear.

The dragon's cave was no more. The roof had finally fallen in on itself, taking a huge chunk out of the grassy clifftop above. A fence that had once held people back from the edge was now half dangling over the precipice. Only the part held up by the iron gate seemed to be still intact. And then, to gasps from those around her, the last section of rock fell too, crushing the gate like it was made of tin foil.

Anything – or anyone – inside wouldn't have stood a chance.

Chapter 25

Mari stood frozen. Her mind raced with awful possibilities. Surely the tiny, fragile dragons could not have survived a rockfall like that? Were they all gone? And was *she* responsible? By bringing them food so they didn't have to leave the cave?

Then an even worse thought hit her.

'Ffion!' she yelled. 'Ffion!'

She had said she would go in to check on the dragons before the collapse. What if she had been inside when the roof came down?

People started turning round to see who was shouting as Mari pushed her way through the throng.

'FFION!'

'I'm here, Mari,' said a voice from behind her.

Mari wrapped her arms around Ffion in an enormous hug, squeezing her as tightly as she possibly could. 'For a minute I thought . . .'

'I know, Mari, I know.'

'What the heck?' said Gareth as he and Dylan arrived on the scene.

'It happened while we were in Cardiff,' said Geraint, coming to join them. 'One of the lifeguards saw it happen. We haven't been here long ourselves. We got here just before *him*.'

Geraint pointed over to a figure at the base of the cliff fall, stumbling around knee-deep in the surf, wailing like a madman. It was Griff.

As they watched, he turned to see them. And now he was bounding towards them with fierce intent.

'Where's my egg? Where is it?'

'It's not *your* egg, Griff,' said Dylan, stepping protectively in front of Mari. 'And it never was.'

'I don't care,' he said. 'I just want it back. Where is it, Mari? I know you've got it.'

'Stay away from her, Griff,' said Nita, stepping out of the crowd to pull him back.

Petra Lunk was there too, and just as agitated as Griff was. 'Are you still *lying* to everyone, Mari?' she hissed, leaning right into her face. 'You know I can't abide lying.'

Mari was a rabbit caught in their headlights. She couldn't think – she was still traumatized by the idea that the dragons in the cave must be –

'We put it back,' Geraint cut in. Everyone turned to look at him. 'The egg. We brought it back here to the cave, where it belongs. And then this happened. So it's under there, somewhere.'

Griff turned to look at the enormous pile of rubble behind them, and then back to face Mari. 'It's not true?' he said. 'Is it?'

Mari's eyes were brimming with tears. All she could think about were the dragons in the cave. The tears began to spill, one by one, down her cheeks.

'IS IT TRUE?' Griff was shouting now.

Mari slowly nodded.

Griff stared deep into her eyes to try and work out whether she was lying. But all he could see was her pain. And he clearly took this to mean that she was telling the truth.

'No,' he whispered. He wheeled away. 'No!' he shouted. 'NO!'

And then he was on his hands and knees, throwing bits of stone this way and that, as if he was going to single-handedly excavate thousands of kilograms of rock.

'It's over,' said Nita, putting her hand on his shoulder. 'All of it. Goodbye, Griff.'

She turned and walked off up the beach on her own.

'And I need to be getting back to Gwyneth,' said Petra. 'I'm sorry about your dragon egg, Mari.

Probably for the best though. Dragons bring out all the crazy folk, don't they?' She gave a funny little wave as she strode off in her pink wellies.

'Time for us to go too, Mari,' said Dylan, resting a hand on her arm.

Mari nodded, remembering the dragon in her pocket. She had to think about Gweeb now.

The ride back to the farmhouse was a sombre affair. For the humans in the car at least. Mari, Dylan and Ffion squeezed into the back seat, and Geraint took up his favoured position in the boot, all with heavy hearts. By contrast, the dragons didn't seem to have a care in the world. Gweeb and Stripe were chasing each other around at such speed that Gareth kept having to duck.

'What's got into you two?' asked Dylan.

'Aren't you at all bothered by this now?' added Mari, holding up Gweeb's stone egg to illustrate her point.

But the dragons clearly weren't. In fact, they had now found the radio and were banging buttons randomly with their snouts, flicking between stations and static.

The chaos was too much for Mari. 'STOP IT!' she yelled.

Everything went quiet. Gweeb turned to look at her quizzically.

'What if there's a reason why they aren't bothered?' said Dylan, all of a sudden.

'What do you mean?' asked Mari.

He reached over and took the egg from her. 'When you found the egg that Gweeb was in, what was it like?'

'I don't follow . . .'

'I mean,' he said, knocking the egg with his knuckles, 'was it like an egg, or was it like stone?'

A smile began to creep across Mari's face. 'So you're saying, maybe that's how dragons' eggs are meant to be?' she said. 'That they have to turn to stone before they can hatch?'

'It would explain why Gweeb doesn't seem worried about it,' said Ffion.

'I like it!' said Gareth from the front seat. 'We can't know how the life cycle of a dragon works, but anything's possible.'

'And what if,' said Mari, warming to the theme now, 'dragons' eggs turn to stone to *protect* them? Maybe they take years to hatch. How long must Gweeb's egg have been locked up inside that cliff face, just waiting for a rockfall to reveal it. Maybe centuries!'

'Could that be why the dragons come to Llanwerydd?' asked Dylan. 'Because the cliffs here are always being worn away. Nesting in the caves could both protect the eggs and, in time, expose them again.'

Mari was getting really excited now. 'And it would mean that all the eggs in the cave would have turned to stone too! And when the cliff collapsed, they wouldn't have been crushed!'

'Then it was all meant to happen!' cried Dylan.

'But what about the little dragons in the cave?' piped up Geraint from the back.

Everyone fell silent. Could those tiny creatures have escaped before the collapse? It was too much to hope for, wasn't it?

'Well I'll be . . .' breathed Gareth, slowing the car to a halt in the lane that led to the farmhouse. 'It's a blooming miracle.'

There, lined up along the overhead cable, as if waiting for them to come home, was the entire flock of dragons.

Chapter 26

In a rush, the dragons took to the air.

'There's *so* many,' Geraint marvelled. 'Can I have my own one now, then?'

'No!' said Mari, Dylan and Ffion at the same time, before bursting into laughter.

Gareth and all four children stood open-mouthed at the sight of the flock swirling overhead. They raced and chased, dived and whirled, relishing the freedom of the domed sky above them. Gweeb, Stripe and Garnet were all there, somewhere in the midst of the great reptilian swarm, but it was impossible to tell them apart from the rest of their extended family.

'I need to get back to the hospital,' said Gareth finally. 'I should drop you two off on the way.'

'Can we stay?' said Geraint. 'Just for a little while?'

'We'll take the bus back,' added Ffion. 'Promise.'

'OK,' he said with a sigh. 'Don't get me into trouble with your parents though.'

He climbed back into the car and trundled off down the lane.

And it was at that moment that a worry dropped lightly into Mari's heart, like a tiny chill.

'This is all part of the cycle too, isn't it?' she said.

The others turned to her, not sure what she meant. 'They come, they nest, and then . . .' She could hardly bring herself to say it. 'Then they go again.'

'Gweeb didn't go last time,' said Dylan. 'Maybe it's different for her. Maybe it will be different for Stripe and Garnet too.'

'I don't know,' mused Mari. 'I get the feeling this is the time that's different. Gweeb didn't really know

Stripe before. She didn't have her own family.' She gazed back up into the sky. 'But now she does.'

As if she could hear Mari speaking, Gweeb broke away from the rest of the flock, and gracefully whirled lower and lower until she was back on Mari's outstretched hand, just as she had been so many times before. Her tail unfurled and coiled itself around Mari's little finger. Mari could feel the lightest squeeze as it did so.

'You're going, aren't you, Gweebie?' she said, bringing her dragon up closer to her face.

Gweeb nuzzled into Mari's palm, and Mari knew that this was goodbye. There was something final about it. Something sad, but also something happy. They had come to the end of their story together, but now Gweeb needed to be part of a story somewhere else.

'Where will you go when you go?' Mari whispered.

Gweeb couldn't tell her. Even if she knew. That mystery would remain, and it was just as well that it did. It meant that no one else would ever find out about Mari's secret dragon. And this would keep her safe. Mari kissed Gweeb lightly on her head.

At that moment Stripe came to land on Dylan's shoulder, and Garnet nestled into Ffion's hand.

'Oh, wow,' said Geraint as another dragon flew down to perch on his index finger. 'Aren't they the most beautiful things in the world?'

'Yes,' said Mari. 'Yes, they are.'

And, with that, all four dragons sprang into the air, followed by the gazes of the four awestruck friends.

They joined up with their flock, until once more they were indistinguishable from the rest. A swirling murmuration of dragons again. The friends stood side by side, arm in arm, to watch. For a few brief moments the flight of dragons whirled back and forth, a final aerobatic show high above the farmhouse, glinting crimson in the evening light. And then they funnelled into an arrow, sure at last of their direction, and wheeled up and away, towards the lighthouse, the clifftops, the sea, and the setting sun.

Epilogue

Mari turned off her desk lamp, thinking for a moment of the tiny creature that used to bask in its light, and turned her attention to rearranging the fossils on her bookshelves. She had to accommodate a rather large new addition to her collection. There, in a little wicker basket she had found at the back of the Welsh dresser, lay a dragon's egg. Gweeb's egg. An egg Mari couldn't even be sure would hatch in her lifetime. But she would make sure it had the best care anyone could offer it until it did. And, most importantly, Dr Griff Griffiths would never, ever find out about it.

There was a crunch of gravel outside, and Mari rushed to her window. Sure enough, a yellow estate car was making its way up the lane to the farmhouse.

'They're back!' she yelled as Dylan came out of his room to meet her on the landing. 'OK?'

'OK.' Dylan nodded. 'Let's go.'

They thundered down the stairs together. Outside, the car slowly came to a halt. Gareth climbed out to open the passenger door for Rhian, then together they went to the back door and leaned in carefully. Soon they had straightened up again, and now Rhian was holding something in her arms, covered in a blanket. She picked her way round the car, making sure not to trip with her precious cargo.

'I want you to say hello to Lindy,' she said, holding out the bundle to Mari.

Mari took the baby in her arms, unsure what to do at first. Dylan looked on with an encouraging smile.

'Hold her like this,' her mum said, showing her how to support the baby's head, and cradle the tiny body in her arms.

Mari looked down just as the baby looked up at her. Emerald-green eyes shone out from beneath the blanket. 'She's beautiful,' she said.

'Yes,' said Rhian. 'Yes, she is.'

'Do you mind if I stroke the baby's head, Rhian?'

It was Dylan asking, not Gareth. Everyone turned to him, and a small tear appeared in Rhian's eye.

'Of course, Dylan,' she said.

Dylan reached out his hand to gently smooth his sister's wispy hair. He smiled up at the rest of his family. Then Mari held out her little finger to her baby sister, and Lindy curled all five of her tiny fingers around it.

'Welcome home,' said Mari.

To find out more about what inspired author

Ed Clarke

read on ...

What is your favourite dinosaur?

My favourite dinosaur when I was growing up was a T-Rex, of course, though now I'm very fond of the ichthyosaur – just like the one that Mary Anning found in Lyme Regis. I think they must have been very beautiful, graceful creatures.

What gave you the inspiration for *Summer of the Dragons*?

Long walks down the beach near my parents' house on the Jurassic coast of Wales. I love it there, and was itching to tell a story about that place. There are dark caves, strange-shaped rocks and crashing waves – all it was missing for a great story was a tiny red dragon!

How long did it take to write *Summer of the Dragons*?

Well, I can usually write about 500 words in an hour if I'm concentrating properly, and there are about 30,000 words in my book. So (if you do the maths) that's sixty hours if I did nothing else. BUT, I do all the planning first, and I do lots more versions after the first one with my editor, copy-editor and proofreader. And I need to sleep sometimes. So all in all it probably works out at about three months.

What is your favourite part of the story?

I don't want to give anything away, but I always enjoy it when Geraint turns up. He was a fun new character to write in this book and has some good scenes, I think!

What was your favourite subject at school?

It was probably history – I always loved imagining the dilemmas of real people in historical situations. How might I have acted in their place? But history also tells us so much about what's happening today – whatever's happening now has almost certainly happened before in some way, and we can learn from the events of the past (if we choose to!).

If you could travel forwards or backwards in time, where would you go and why?

I'd love to go back to Elizabethan times and meet Shakespeare – he's such a mysterious figure in many ways, and it would be fascinating to find out what kind of person he really was. And ask him for a few writing tips!

What do you like about science?

I love that science is about being curious about the world around us, about asking questions and trying to find the answers. And it can start anywhere – in your bedroom, in the playground, in the park – you don't need a laboratory. You just need to start with a question. How does this work? Where does this come from? Why does this happen? They're the same questions you ask yourself when you're writing a story too!

If you could make one scientific discovery that would change the world, what would it be and why?

Right now, I don't think there's anything more important than the way we're treating our environment, so I'd want to discover something that could help our planet. Like some kind of super tree that sucks up all the pollution we create. Or a cheap clean-energy source that would stop everyone creating the pollution in the first place, like a mega solar panel in space that beams back all the electricity we would ever need.

Do you have any pets?

My daughters have two rabbits called Midnight and Betty. Fortunately, we don't have to keep them a secret, as they're a lot bigger than Gweeb and would be much harder to hide in my pocket.

What is the best thing about being an author?

I think it's a real privilege to be allowed to write stories that are read by a lot of children. And when that story excites or moves or touches someone you've never even met, in the way you dared hope when you were writing it, that's by far the biggest thrill.

About the Author

When Ed Clarke isn't writing for kids, he is a film and television executive and producer, working with writers to make dramas for grown-ups. He recently moved to East Sussex with his wife and two young daughters, whose constant pleas for pets were finally answered. They were only slightly disappointed to get rabbits instead of dragons.